Lord Storm jumped down and came around to her side of the carriage and held up his arms to help her down.

Well, he had meant to behave. But as she bent forward in the moonlight, he saw the deep valley between her perfect breasts. She fell down into his arms and he clasped her tightly.

His arms seemed full of woman. Emily pressed against his chest, long slim legs against his legs, hair tumbling down, dark midnight hair clean and scented with lavender water, eyes gazing up into his, mouth bewildered, soft and pleading . . .

He trapped her mouth under his and the night went whirling away . . .

DUKE'S DIAMONDS

MARION CHESNEY

FAWCETT CREST • NEW YORK

A Fawcett Crest Book
Published by Ballantine Books

Copyright © 1982 by Marion Chesney

ISBN 0-449-20085-X

Manufactured in the United States of America

First Ballantine Books Edition: January 1983

For Lynne Shapiro
with love

Chapter One

"The fact is, my dear Duke, we have a great deal to be thankful for," Miss Emily Winters said severely.

And Duke, a great shaggy mongrel, stared up at her out of his rather close-set, mean-looking eyes and wagged his ridiculous plume of a tail.

"But sometimes," Emily went on, looking with large, sad eyes across the expanse of lawn to the mellow brick facade of Manley Court, "it is very hard to remember. If Sir Peregrine dies—and it seems more than likely he will, and very soon, too—then you and I, Duke, will be looking for a home."

Duke parted his black lips and yellow teeth in an idiotic grin and buried his narrow head in her lap.

A chill November wind sighed through the bare branches of the lime trees that bordered the drive and ruffled the waters of the ornamental lake.

Emily was a distant relative of Sir Peregrine Manley, "about two hundred times removed," as Sir Peregrine's sister, Harriet, was wont to remark.

But at least that acid comment was better than the openly expressed view of Sir Peregrine's other kin, which was that Emily was no distant relative at all but one of the old man's by-blows. Since Emily herself did not know the names of her parents, she could do little to stand up for herself.

She was seventeen years of age and, until six months ago, she had known no other life than that of the Baxtead Orphanage. It was not an orphanage for destitute children but for unwanted children, placed there by relatives who did not want to house them. Her fees were paid through a lawyer's office in London. But the lawyers refused to disclose the secret of her birth, simply saying that a relative of the Manley family paid for her keep at the orphanage and had requested that his name be kept secret.

Just before Emily's seventeenth birthday, Sir Peregrine Manley had arrived at the orphanage. He was a florid, gouty, tetchy gentleman in his fifties. How he had come to learn of Emily's existence he would never say, but he had looked her over with his watery blue eyes and had announced he was taking her to his home because he had a job for her.

The patronesses of the orphanage had given her up without a murmur, and Emily had gone with him very unwillingly indeed, having been brought up on scarifying tales from the other girls about the peculiar lusts of gentlemen.

But the job turned out to be ludicrous, although Sir Peregrine was perfectly in earnest about it. She was to be keeper and companion to his dog, Duke. She was to spend her days and nights with the dog, since Sir Peregrine believed that one of his relatives planned to poison the animal.

At first Emily was inclined to sympathize with the relatives, since Duke was hideously spoiled. He lay in the best chairs and no one was allowed to move him. He blocked the heat from the fire in the evenings by standing in front of it. He loved hiding in dark corners and bounding out to nip an unwary ankle.

But after the rigors of the orphanage, Manley Court had seemed like a dream with its well-appointed rooms and beautiful gardens. Emily had set herself to win the affections of Duke. At first it was difficult, and her future hung in the balance. Duke had eaten her only pair of slippers and she had smacked him, and, like a spoiled child, he had gone whimpering to Sir Peregrine. It was only when Emily had discovered that the dog was overweight, his coat dull, that he lacked exercise and was badly in need of a good staple diet, that things took a turn for the better. She walked miles with the mongrel panting happily at her heels, and after the third walk, Duke became her slave. Emily was apt to think that a devoted Duke was every bit as repellent as an antagonistic Duke, since the animal had a creeping sycophantic manner, but Sir Peregrine was delighted, and that was all that mattered.

And so her life would have been quite perfect had it not been for the other members of the household. First, there was Sir Peregrine's sister, Harriet, a thin, acid spinster with a razor tongue and a jealous eye. Then there was Sir Peregrine's brother, James, a thin, ascetic clergyman with a knack of making everyone in general and Emily in particular feel they were not good enough for this world or, for that matter, the next. And finally, there were his two nieces, Fanny and Betty, who were not orphans but who had been sent along by their parents as sort of permanent house guests at Manley Court in the hope that Sir Peregrine would die soon and leave them some of his wealth.

That, in fact, was what they were all waiting for—with the exception of Emily. The Manleys were waiting for Sir

Peregrine to die. Aside from Manley Court and its profitable estates, he possessed a fortune in diamonds.

It was not that he was so very old. He was fifty-four. But a long life of self-indulgence, bachelorhood, bad temper, and utter selfishness had left their mark on Sir Peregrine's health.

He was a prey to gout, and his heart was said to be bad. He had already had two seizures, from which he had miraculously recovered. The doctor had prophesied that a third would kill him.

In recent weeks, he had been confined to his bedchamber quite a lot, leaving Emily to the mercy of his relatives. They had been quite charming to her at first, fully expecting her stay to last only a week. But the growing affections of Duke and consequently the growing affections of Sir Peregrine had made them eye Emily with open hostility. As far as they were concerned, she was a threat to the inheritance that they had begun to look on as their own. Emily sighed, and Duke slobbered his tongue over her hand and grinned at her again.

Sir Peregrine had promised to be present at dinner that evening, as his neighbor, Bartholomew Storm—Lord Storm—had returned from the Peninsular Wars and had been invited as guest of honor. He was rumored to be extremely rich and handsome—and unmarried. Fanny and Betty had been in a flutter all morning and had wandered around with their hair in curl papers, planning elaborate toilets to dazzle this possible suitor.

They had tried their hardest to have Emily excluded from the dinner, going so far as to tell the housekeeper that Emily would have a tray in her room. But the housekeeper had referred the matter to Sir Peregrine, who had gleefully countermanded the order. He loved his relatives' jealousy of Emily and did everything he could to make it worse. It gave him a feeling of power to have all these people vying for his affections, although he knew very well they were only after his money.

After having delightedly mused on the joys of upsetting them further, he recalled that he had asked his young cousin, Clarissa Singleton, to stay, and with any luck she would arrive in time for dinner.

Mrs. Singleton was a widow of considerable beauty and charm. Sir Peregrine considered her to be like one of his finest diamonds. Glittering, beautiful, and extremely hard.

In any case, Fanny and Betty's twittering spite and sister Harriet's acid remarks had driven Emily to take refuge in the park. They were all very greedy people, she mused. Harriet possessed a fortune of her own; James Manley was rector of Baxtead and had a rich living; and Fanny and Betty's parents owned considerable property. But one thing was sure. They all wanted the Manley fortune and were prepared to go to any lengths to get it.

Emily found herself wondering about this mysterious Lord Storm. He was accounted "quite young." Perhaps he would be someone merry and cheerful who would treat her kindly.

She certainly could not dream of matrimony to a lord. She was some sort of legal parcel which had been delivered to the orphanage and then to Sir Peregrine. As far as the law was concerned, she had no say in anything, and Emily had come sadly to the conclusion that she must be illegitimate; otherwise the lawyers and the orphanage would surely have told her the identity of her parents.

She was unaware that there was an added reason for Fanny's and Betty's spite and their determination, now foiled, to have her excluded from the dinner party.

Emily was quite beautiful. She had masses of jet-black hair, which curled naturally. Her skin was extremely fair, the cheeks a delicate pink. Her eyes were a wide and candid blue with a dark ring around the iris and very slightly tilted at the corners, giving her a somewhat Slavonic appearance. She had a slim figure, a neat ankle, and a deep bosom.

Of course, the ladies of the household had taken steps to extinguish some of this "blowsiness," as Harriet put it. Her hair was severely scraped back and confined in a knot at her neck. Her gowns were of the simplest style, since she was not a very good needlewoman and had been presented with some lengths of cloth and told to make her own.

It was not only the cruel remarks of the ladies of Manley Court that had upset her, thought Emily, but a certain something inside her, a frustrated yearning for kindness and warmth and laughter.

And mixed up with all these mixed emotions was a feeling of rebellion. She tried to remind herself that she was a penniless orphan and that she should be grateful for *any* charity, but she longed for balls and jewels and pretty dresses with all her feminine heart.

Emily suddenly shivered, feeling stiff and cold. She arose from the fallen log she had been sitting on and began to walk slowly across the lawns toward the house. She seized Duke's collar just in time. His ruff had gone up and he had shown every sign of being about to mangle an adventurous deer that was ambling placidly along.

Emily began to wonder what on earth she should wear that evening and if there was any way in which she could prettify her meager wardrobe.

She was still deep in thought when she reached her room. Duke had a special bed made for him, in the corner by the fire. But in his usual perverse way, he ignored it completely and stretched his muddy paws luxuriously out on the counterpane of Emily's bed.

Emily pulled her one silk gown out of the closet and looked at it in despair. It had been made for her by a friend at the orphanage and had the merit of being in the latest fashion, with a low bodice and little puffed sleeves. The skirt fell straight from the high Empire waistline and ended in two deep flounces. But the color was a sort of streaky, muddy brown, which is why a great bolt of it had been so generously donated to the orphanage.

It was then that she noticed that the curtains in her room were edged with gold silk fringe. . . .

Emily was to make her entrance in the drawing room some twenty minutes late, having been sent by Harriet to look for a mythical work basket that that lady was supposed to have mislaid.

Emily was to be seated at the table well away from Lord Storm, but Harriet was determined to take care of that traditional half hour in the drawing room before dinner when the ladies and gentlemen assembled for a drink.

Harriet had ranged herself on the side of Fanny and Betty, secretly feeling that if one of these young ladies could entrap Lord Storm, it would take their minds off the inheritance. She had reckoned, however, without the arrival of Clarissa Singleton.

From the top of her well-coiffeured head to the points of her bronze kid slippers, Mrs. Singleton was the very picture of modish perfection. Her red-gold hair blazed above a perfect oval face, painted with the hand of an artist.

Harriet had not been present when Mrs. Singleton arrived, and so she met her for the first time when she walked into the drawing room. Dressed in puce, which matched her complexion, Harriet, who had felt very elegant in the privacy of her bedchamber, felt old-fashioned and dowdy beside the glittering Clarissa. Why, even her brother, the reverend James, was making a cake of himself over the woman.

Both Fanny and Betty were attired in flimsy muslin

gowns decorated with a great quantity of ribbons. They were sulking over in a corner as far from the merry widow as they could get. Lord Storm had not yet arrived.

Sir Peregrine was ensconced in an armchair by the fire with his gouty foot up on a stool. His face was a muddy color and his breathing harsh and rapid, but his eyes sparkled maliciously as he looked from one face to the other.

"Where's Emily?" he barked.

Harriet bit her lip. Emily was bound to arrive and blurt out her reason for being late. "I sent her to look for my work basket," she snapped. "Time she earned her keep."

"You ain't got a work basket," said Sir Peregrine. "Never could sew a seam. Never will. Anyway, it ain't any use you worrying about Emily being competition when we've got Clarissa here."

"*Sweet* uncle," murmured Clarissa. "Always the flatterer!"

Fanny and Betty bridled in their corner and tossed their heads. They did not like being outclassed by Clarissa. In truth, both Fanny and Betty were very well in their way. Although Fanny was a year older, being twenty to Betty's nineteen, they could have been taken for twins.

Each had fat glossy ringlets in profusion, wide dark eyes, a long nose, and a mouth small enough to meet the demands of fashion. Each was inordinately proud of her tiny mouth and would make it smaller by speaking in sort of prunes-and-prisms voices, warbling her native wood-notes wild out of a little hole prissed up in the center of the mouth.

They should have studied their Aunt Harriet's face to see what could happen to a lady in later years who had pursed her mouth all her life to meet the dictates of fashion. Harriet's mouth was surrounded by a radius of wrinkles. She always looked as if she were about to spit.

"Do you think Lord Storm has had an accident?" asked Harriet, her eyes gloomily noting that Clarissa had dampened her gown of gold tissue so that it would cling more closely to her voluptuous figure.

"Not he," said Sir Peregrine. "Tell 'em to set back the dinner quarter of an hour."

Lord Storm had in fact just arrived, and, finding a servant had left the main door a little ajar, he pushed it open and let himself into the hall, placing his hat and cane on a side table and looking about him.

He was about to ring for a servant when he noticed a beautiful girl descending the staircase. She was holding a candle in a brass candlestick and had an evil-looking mongrel at her heels.

At the same moment, Emily caught sight of him and stopped on the half-landing, looking down. At first glance he looked like the most handsome man she had ever seen. His hair was worn longer than the current fashion and was tied by a black velvet ribbon at the nape of his neck. His hair was so blond it was nearly white, and his face was deeply tanned. He had light-gray eyes under heavy drooping lids, a patrician nose, and a square chin. He was wearing a swallow-tailed coat with the tight-fitting evening trousers pioneered by Brummell that fitted the leg like a second skin and reached to just above the ankle, displaying an expanse of striped silk stocking.

His cravat was intricately folded and starched, and a single sapphire pin blazed against its snowy whiteness.

He stood watching her in silence until she became aware that she had been staring at him and blew out her candle—for the hall was brightly lit—and made her way down the stairs toward him.

Her silk gown rustled about her, and the gold fringe from the curtains that she had used to embellish it fluttered as she moved.

He made her a deep bow and said in an attractive, husky voice, "I am Storm. I was about to ring for a servant, but perhaps you may save me the trouble, Miss . . . ?"

"Winters, my lord."

"Miss Winters, will you show me to the drawing room?"

Emily swept him a low curtsy and murmured, "Certainly, my lord."

She fought down a little twinge of disappointment. His eyes were hard and cold, and he seemed very haughty.

He held out his arm, and she tentatively laid her gloved hand on his sleeve, indicating the drawing room with a little nod of her head.

A footman suddenly materialized and rushed to throw open the doors for them, and Lord Storm, not knowing whether this young lady was a guest of the house or no, gave the footman both their names.

"Miss Winters and Lord Storm," announced the footman.

The party in the drawing room, with the exception of Sir Peregrine, rose to their feet. From the looks on the ladies' faces, Emily realized she was being damned for having stolen a march on them.

The drawing room was a blaze of gold and crimson; gilt furniture with crimson upholstery, gold-painted ceiling, crimson curtains, and two fine Waterford chandeliers.

"Come in! Come in!" cried Sir Peregrine. "No need to stand on formality, heh? You're name's Bartholomew, I believe."

"My friends of long standing call me Bart," said his lordship pleasantly. "But others address me by my title. You may call me Storm."

Insufferable, thought Emily, who had detached herself from him at the earliest opportunity.

"Hey, well, well," said Sir Peregrine, looking slightly taken aback. "I'd better make the company known to you. This here is m'sister, Harriet, and the thin one in the dog collar is m'brother, James. He'll save your soul for you, heh?'' He let out a bellow of laughter while Lord Storm eyed him coldly.

''And the ladies?'' queried Lord Storm in a tone that plainly implied Sir Peregrine should have introduced them first.

''Heh, what? Eh, yes. Well, this here dasher is m'cousin, Clarissa Singleton. And those two charmers over there are m'nieces, Fanny and Betty Kipling. And now, since you've met everyone, we'll have some refreshment.''

The ladies clustered around the distinguished visitor. Lord Storm raised his quizzing glass and looked pointedly in Emily's direction. ''And Miss Winters is . . . ?''

''Dog's companion,'' said Harriet with a harsh laugh. Emily stooped quickly and patted Duke's head. ''Oh, by the by,'' said Harriet, ''did you find my work basket, Miss Winters? Got to earn your keep, you know.''

Before Emily could reply, Sir Peregrine said gleefully, ''Pay her no heed, Emmy. She ain't got a work basket. Just out to humiliate you. I got Emmy from the orphanage,'' went on Sir Peregrine. ''She looks after Duke.''

''The duke?'' asked Lord Storm. ''Which one?''

''My dog Duke, that's who,'' said Sir Peregrine. ''Only one who ain't after my money. They're all after my money, 'cept Emmy, which is strange, since she's the only one who could do with it.''

A stunned and embarrassed silence met these family revelations.

''Miss Winters is not then a relative of yours,'' said Lord Storm, looking over the heads of his court of ladies to where Emily was standing.

''Oh, she's some sort o' kin,'' said Sir Peregrine carelessly.

''Your lordship should know that poor relations are a

feature and fixture of every gentleman's home," said Clarissa Singleton merrily.

"Indeed I do," he said, smiling down at her. "Fortunately, humiliating them openly in company is not."

Clarissa flushed.

"Tell us about the fighting in the Peninsula," fluted Fanny, delighted at Clarissa's set-down.

"I do not like to talk about the war."

There was another silence while everyone drank feverishly and wondered what to say next.

Lord Storm began to stroll across the room toward Emily. Emily tried not to shrink back. She would have preferred to be ignored.

"What kind of animal is that?" demanded his lordship, leveling his quizzing glass at Duke. Duke began to growl softly, and his ruff went up.

"Duke is a mongrel," said Emily, amazed at the calmness of her own voice, for she was beginning to find Lord Storm quite terrifying.

His cold eyes looked down at Duke. Duke slowly curled his lips back from his teeth and stared up at Lord Storm with a reddish glint in his close-set eyes.

"Amazing," said Lord Storm, letting his quizzing glass drop. "I find it very strange. I consider the place for a dog to be in the kennel and the place for a cat to be in the kitchen. Obviously you do not agree, Sir Peregrine. I trust Miss Winters is fond of animals?"

"Yes, my lord," said Emily, staring at the floor.

"Dinner is served," announced the butler, and a sigh of relief rose from the assembled party.

Sir Peregrine was carried in by two footmen. Lord Storm followed next, with Harriet on his arm; Clarissa Singleton came next, on the arm of James Manley; Betty and Fanny escorted each other; and Emily and Duke brought up the rear.

Since dining in the sun was considered far more unpleasant than gloom or chill, the Manley Court dining room faced northeast and was freezingly cold. With its heavy somber furniture it was as solemn as a courtroom. A huge oil painting of a carcass with its innards hanging out embellished one wall, and on the other a highly colored saint was shedding scarlet blood as he was flogged by muscular Romans in bright-blue togas. At the end of the room, a small coal fire sent all its heat straight up the chimney.

Lord Storm was placed next to Harriet, with Clarissa Singleton on his other side. Sir Peregrine took the opposite end of the table from his sister, and the rest arranged themselves as best they could.

A smaller dining room was usually used for family meals, and this particular room had not been used for two years. It had an enormous oblong table, meant to seat a whole banquet of people. The party found themselves a long way away from each other and realized they would have to shout to be heard by the person next to them.

No sooner was the turtle soup served—thick or clear—than Mr. James Manley arose to say grace. Sir Peregrine rapped lightly on his plate, and Emily's heart sank. That rap meant Sir Peregrine was not in the eating vein and therefore James had permission to make the grace as long as he wanted. Although James was a minister of the Church of England, Emily had often thought he might have been happier had he chosen one of those sects that delighted in preaching hellfire. She was sure his histrionic abilities were wasted on the Anglican church.

James took a deep breath and began. "Dear Father, we beseech thee . . ."

Just then, Emily felt Duke's wet nose pushed into her hand. This was his signal that he wanted to go out. But how could she rise in the middle of grace? Emily gave the dog a little rap on the nose, which was her signal that he could not go out, and he slunk away under the table.

The turtle soup began to cool on the plates as James went on and on, working himself into a religious sweat.

"So my dear brethren, we must work and strive and pray to be worthy of the food we see before us. Strike humility into our hearts this evening, oh Father, so that we may kneel and say . . . damn! Hell! Blast! Rot it! Rot it! Oh, double, double, *double rot!*"

Everyone looked up in surprise. James was weaving his head around inside its clerical collar like a demented tortoise. "Anythin' the matter, James?" asked Sir Peregrine.

"No!" screamed James. And in a quieter voice, he hurriedly said, "Amen," and bent his head over his soup. Emily, looking for Duke, leaned back in her chair a little. And then she saw the cause of the rector's distress. He had one silk-stockinged leg stuck out beside his chair. A pool of liquid lay on the floor at his heel, and the silk of his stocking was damp.

Oh, Duke! thought Emily in distress. Couldn't you have waited? She knew well that James would not dare tell the reason for his outburst. Sir Peregrine would brook no criticism whatsoever of his dog.

She looked around the table, hoping that no one had noticed. Lord Storm caught her eye and gave her a mocking, teasing smile. That smile so changed his face, made him so blindingly handsome, that poor Emily felt her insides tremble. She breathlessly reminded herself that his lordship was rude and haughty and overbearing and stared fixedly at her plate.

When she looked up again, Lord Storm was listening to Harriet, who was shouting about plumbing. His face was a mask of boredom, and Emily was able to concentrate on her dinner and at the same time try to persuade herself that she was not freezing to death. Mrs. Singleton's white shoulders were turning a delicate shade of blue. Duke was standing, blocking the fire.

What an unconscionably long meal it was!

Remove followed remove.

The turtle soup was followed by turbot with lobster sauce, followed by mutton, followed by turkey, and then the game began to circulate—grouse, woodcock, partridge, snipe, and all with the accompanying punch, hock, white hermitage, sparkling moselle, and burgundy. Then came creams and jellies and puffs and pastries, and still the meal was not over.

"Do try a little *fondieu*," Fanny begged Lord Storm.

"What on earth is that?" shouted his lordship, since Fanny was about an acre of polished mahogany away.

"Miss Kipling means *fondue*," called Emily before she could help herself.

"That's what I said," snapped Fanny, waving away a water ice.

At long last, Harriet arose to lead the ladies from the room and so leave the gentlemen to their port and all those nasty "warm" stories that ladies were not supposed to hear.

Emily decided to make her escape, but Harriet said coldly, "I want a word with you, Miss Winters," and so Emily had to follow her meekly into the drawing room.

"Now, Miss Winters," began Harriet as the other ladies rushed to warm themselves at the fire, "I think it is high time to remind you of your place. You are a penniless incumbent. You are tolerated as a kind of kennel boy to that disgusting animal. I fear my poor brother is not long for this world, and when he departs it, you, miss, depart Manley Court and that excuse for a hound goes with you. Do I make myself plain?"

"You are indeed very plain as it is," said Emily with a

rare burst of spirit. "Do not, I pray you, endeavor to make matters worse."

"Jade!" fumed Harriet, quite beside herself with rage. Duke ambled over and stood looking up at Harriet, his ruff rising ominously.

"Furthermore, you have no right to be aping your betters by wearing silk. That gown is too rich for you, miss. Furthermore, you were very foward in encouraging Lord Storm's advances—for gentlemen will always make bold advances when their object is not marriage. Furthermore . . ."

But Duke decided he had heard enough. He seized Harriet's skirt in his teeth and began to worry it.

"Shoo!" screamed Harriet, pulling her skirt one way as Duke began to pull it the other. "A pox on you, you hairy fleabag! You useless monster!"

There was a great rending, and Duke sat back triumphantly on his haunches with a good piece of Harriet's skirt in his teeth. Fanny and Betty began to scream as well, and Mrs. Singleton calmly helped herself to brandy.

Emily seized Duke by the collar and dragged him from the room. "Oh, you *impossible* dog!" She sighed. "But how can I scold you when I am so in need of a champion? We'll go for a walk and hide until they are all gone to bed."

Duke, hearing that magic word "walk," followed her eagerly up the stairs.

Once in her room, Emily debated what to wear, for she knew the night outside was probably frigid. She rapidly changed into an old wool gown and a shabby mantle and wrapped a heavy shawl around her head. After a moment's hesitation, she pulled the quilt from the bed and slung it over her arm.

She led Duke quietly down the back stairs and out into the night.

White frost glittered on the spiky grass and rimed the

trees on the lawn. The air was still and cold, and winter stars blazed in the blackness of the sky above. Duke ran around and around and around in a sort of ecstasy of freedom. One would have thought he had been chained up in a kennel for days.

Emily walked across the great expanse of lawn that fronted the house until she was at the edge of the home wood. There was her favorite log, near the drive and far enough from the house to allow her to sit peacefully and dream.

Duke plunged into the wood in search of rabbits, and Emily wrapped herself up in the quilt and gazed up at the stars and dreamed of having a cozy little home to go where she could call her soul her own.

After some time, she noticed a carriage being brought around to the front door. A figure jumped up into the box and shouted something in the way of adieu, and then the coach started to roll down the drive toward her.

Lord Storm was driving himself. She watched as he approached, seeing the glimmer of his face in the faint starlight. To her surprise, he reined in his horses and climbed down. Emily waited breathlessly, huddled in the quilt, sure that he could not see her. But he shouted to his tiger to hold the reins and then began to walk toward her.

Chapter Two

When he was quite close, he paused and made her a courtly bow, then, without waiting for permission, sat down on the log beside her.

He removed his curly-brimmed beaver and placed it on the grass at his feet. The starlight glinted on the thick fair whiteness of his hair and glinted in his eyes as he looked down at her.

"What are you doing here, Miss Winters?" he asked.

Emily looked up at Lord Storm with a certain degree of irritation. For she had decided his lordship was one of *them*, that little army of people put on this earth for the sole purpose of baiting her.

"I wanted to be alone, my lord."

"I cannot blame you," he said lazily. "The company was rude, boring, and dreary. I shall not call again."

"And your lordship was *not* rude, boring, and dreary?"

He looked at her with some hauteur. "Do you not think that you go a great deal too far, Miss Winters?"

"Oh, you mean, why don't I remember my place," said Emily. She gave a little sigh that expelled itself in the frosty air in a cloud. "It does not matter, you see. I am tolerated by Sir Peregrine because of the dog. When he dies, his sister says she will send me from the house. She and the others are forced to tolerate me because of Sir Peregrine. I realized tonight when she was berating me in the drawing room that I really did not need to guard my tongue. In the common way, I am polite and civil. But of late, the provocation has been great."

"Who were your parents?" he asked abruptly.

"I do not know. I am some relative of the Manleys, that is all I do know. My stay at the orphanage was paid for by some relative who left express instructions that his name not be revealed to me."

"And what will you do when they turn you out?"

"I really do not know," said Emily wearily, "and at this time of night, sir, I confess I do not really care."

"Odso! Then what shall we do with pretty Emily?"

His voice was suddenly warm and caressing.

"It is not your concern," she said breathlessly.

He took her hand in his and, turning it over, pressed a kiss into the palm. "I could make it my business," he said, smiling down into her eyes.

The sudden aura of strong sexuality that seemed to emanate from him had the effect of striking her dumb. Her lips parted in bewilderment. Her mouth was young and soft and almost not quite formed.

Before she could find her voice, he had bent his head and trapped her mouth in a kiss. His lips were cool and firm, and therefore she found the violent reaction of the rest of her body quite unaccountable.

For one brief second, she realized all her churning thoughts and frustrations had found a focus, and it was as if some great rising tide of passion in her body had just reached her lips. When her brain screamed warning, she pushed him away, appalled at having been so near the edge of surrender.

The night was bitterly cold. His eyes were once more hard and cruel.

"Leave me alone, my lord," said Emily in a cold, thin voice. "I may not know my parents, I may be penniless, but that should not give you license to take liberties."

"I subjected you to an excess of civility, that was all," said Lord Storm, standing up and drawing on his York tan driving gloves, then stooping to pick up his hat.

He wheeled about and strode away from her. She did not wait to see him reach his carriage, but stood up on shaky legs, calling for Duke, who came scrambling helter-skelter out of the woods. Huddling the quilt about her, she began to run toward the house, the shaggy dog loping at her heels.

It was only after he reached home and was sitting in front of his library fire that Lord Storm was calm enough to understand he was more furious with himself than he was with Emily.

The library smelled comfortingly of Russia leather and cigar smoke and brandy. Only a slight twinge in his leg reminded him of the wound that had sent him home from the wars.

After some hard thought, he decided that he had been sure she had been sitting on that log by the drive in order to waylay him. Looking back, he realized she had simply been sitting there to escape from the house and its inhabitants. But, damn it all, she should be aware that her lack of birth and social status laid her wide open to familiarities such as he had inflicted upon her. It was the way of the world. He was not to blame. But he had to confess himself annoyed at her rejection. It was the first he could remember.

His fortune and his title had brought the ladies in droves to his feet. It had also, he reflected, brought every creepy crawly counter-jumper, toad-eater, and pushing Cit to his door. He had been able to be shot of most of them during his brief army career as a captain in a cavalry regiment. It was a pity Miss Winters would obviously not consider the post of mistress. It was, of course, out of the question to consider her as a wife. Lord Storm placed himself on too high a form to dream of allying himself to any but the finest of the top ten thousand.

Well, he would not see her again, since he had no intention of ever returning to Manley Court.

And yet . . . and yet . . . her lips had been delicious. With a great effort, he firmly banished Miss Emily Winters from his mind and turned his thoughts to Clarissa Singleton. A trifle shrewish, but a beauty for all that, and a kind of beauty that usually attracted him. He liked his women brittle and sophisticated.

Of course, they were all waiting like vultures for the old man to die. Except Miss Winters. Damn Miss Winters. Think of something else.

Emily lay in bed dreaming of Lord Storm. In her dreams, they were lying beside a river in each other's arms. It was a warm, lazy, sensuous dream. His eyes were warm with love, and his mouth was approaching closer and closer. . . .

She awoke with a jerk and then froze at the feel of the warm body pressed against her back.

She whirled around and found herself face to face with Duke, who was lying on the next pillow. He yawned sleepily and licked her nose.

"Get out of my bed this minute," said Emily crossly.

She pushed and pushed until Duke toppled sulkily off the edge and crawled off to his own bed by the fire, where he lay watching her moodily.

There was something almost reptilian about his narrow, smooth, mean head, which contrasted so oddly with his shaggy black-and-gold coat. Emily often wondered whether Sir Peregrine was as devoted to his dog as he liked to make out. He hardly saw the animal. After some thought she had decided that Sir Peregrine used Duke in the same way as he used herself—to irritate his family.

Her status was in its way worse than that of a servant. Only look how low Lord Storm had rated her. She burned with humiliation when she remembered her own brief passionate response to his caress. That was what came of not really being a lady. She would be on her guard next time she saw him. But then she would not see him again. He did not give the impression of a man who wished to see any of the inmates of Manley Court again.

Since the day after the dinner party, Sir Peregrine's health had begun to fail. It was not that he had any of his usual apoplectic fits. He simply seemed to begin to waste away.

He rarely emerged from his room, and although his family would have liked to bully Emily more than they did, they were afraid of Sir Peregrine's tale-bearing servants. But just when the end seemed as if it must be near, he made a miraculous recovery and confounded his relatives by appearing hale and hearty at the breakfast table one morning.

It was too much for Betty and Fanny. Mama must be told they were wasting their time, and soon they took their departure, to Emily's infinite relief. Clarissa Singleton remained.

And then one snowy morning, out of the blue, came an invitation from Lord Storm. Sir Peregrine and members of his household were invited to attend a supper. There would be dancing and cards afterward.

Emily had tried very hard not to think of Lord Storm since that last evening, but somehow his face always seemed to be floating before her eyes. Clarissa Singleton promptly departed for town to choose a new dress especially for the occasion. Harriet surprised everyone by opting to go with her. James was back at his rectory. So for three blessed days Emily practically had the house to herself. Or rather, that was what it felt like, although Sir Peregrine was present, not to mention a whole army of servants.

The day before the supper party was chilly, with the park glittering under a light fall of snow. Sir Peregrine suddenly announced he would like to take the air with Emily and Duke. Leaning heavily on a cane and wrapped up to the eyebrows, he hobbled forth. Duke seemed fully aware of the honor being done him and raced around and around, throwing up clouds of powdery snow.

The sun was glittering and gold against a bank of ominous clouds—a sure sign of a storm on the way.

''Well, Emmy,'' wheezed Sir Peregrine, ''better'n the orphanage, heh?''

''Yes, indeed,'' said Emily politely.

''There was a little silence while they shuffled in the direction of the lake.

''*Why* did you take me from the orphanage, Sir Peregrine?'' asked Emily.

''Why, to look after Duke, don't you see?''

''But, I mean, why *me*? How did you learn of my existence?''

''Through the family, o' course.''

Emily stopped and turned pleading eyes to his. ''Oh, Sir Peregrine. You must know who my parents were. Or at least you must know the name of the relatives who paid for my keep in the orphanage. Please tell me!''

''Can't,'' mumbled Sir Peregrine, avoiding her gaze.

"Gave my word. Secret, don't you see. No, don't ask any more. Shan't tell you."

They had reached the border of the lake with its pretty rotunda on the island in the middle shining in the glaring sunlight.

Sir Peregrine stooped and picked up a stick. "Here, boy!" he shouted to Duke. "Fetch!"

He threw it into the waters of the lake and laughed like a child as Duke plunged into the icy waters and swam after it.

"He'll catch a cold!" said Emily. "You should not . . ."

"Tol-rol," said Sir Peregrine, waggling his fingers disdainfully. "My hounds are out in all weathers, and not one o' 'em comes to harm."

Duke bounded to the shore, carrying the stick between his teeth, and dropped it at Sir Peregrine's gouty feet.

"Aha! What! Good boy! Fetch!" And Sir Peregrine threw the stick back in the lake again.

Emily bit her lip. She wanted to point out to Sir Peregrine that his hounds were hardened to all weathers and did not sleep in specially made beds or lounge in front of the drawing-room fire.

The bank of clouds closed overhead and blotted out the sun. Tiny pellets of snow began to whip into their faces.

"Duke's in trouble!" shouted Emily, as Sir Peregrine was shuffling about to point himself in the direction of the house.

The dog was struggling in the middle of the lake. He appeared to be caught on something. He gave a long yowl of distress, and his head went under.

Almost without thought, Emily ran into the water and began to wade out to where Duke had disappeared. She could not swim; she prayed it would not get any deeper. Weeds clung around her ankles and wrapped their tentacles around her sodden skirts.

"Come back, you fool!" shouted Sir Peregrine.

The water was up to Emily's chin now, and she thought that Duke was dead, but his head suddenly broke the surface again less than a yard in front of her. Reaching out her arm, Emily caught his collar in a firm grip.

Duke was too tired to struggle, which was the saving of him. She felt under the water and found strands of weed wound around one of his back legs, and she tore at them until she managed to get the leg free. And then, towing the limp animal behind her, she struggled toward the shore.

She sledged Duke through the thin ice at the edge and up on the snowy bank, then looked down at his now unconscious form helplessly. She bent down and began to pump his paws backward and forward in the mad hope that she could reanimate his circulation. He suddenly vomited a great burst of lake water and began to shiver.

"Good Duke. Fine Duke," muttered Emily, heaving his huge body up into her arms.

She found herself shivering uncontrollably. A burst of temper did a great deal to give her the necessary energy to carry the animal toward the house, for Sir Peregrine had callously walked off without waiting to see if either of them lived or died.

The butler, Rogers, saw her approach and sent two footmen out to relieve her of her burden. Duke was hustled upstairs and rubbed down with warm towels.

The housekeeper, Mrs. Otley, bustled in at the head of an army of servants, some to fill a bath for Emily, others to pile extra blankets on her bed.

"That was a brave thing you did, Miss Winters," said Mrs. Otley, "and you are appreciated by the staff, if not by others."

Rogers arrived with a bottle of brandy on a tray and the news that the kennel master would arrive to look at Duke as soon as Miss Winters was bathed and changed.

Emily made quick work of her bath and felt much better when she was attired in a smart plain walking gown that she had never seen before. She wondered where Mrs. Otley had found it, for it was a perfect fit.

The kennel master, James Balfour, was ushered in. He was attired in a bright-green plush shooting jacket with innumerable pockets and the most dilapidated pair of white moleskins Emily had ever seen thrust into drab horn-buttoned gaiters and hobnailed shoes.

He examined Duke, who was lying breathing rapidly. He looked at his dry nose, prized open an eye, and looked at the red and feverish eyeball.

"Shoot 'im," he said.

"What?" said Emily, who had been watching this performance anxiously.

"Beggin' yer parding, mum, but e's not long for this here world. Shoot 'im. Most merciful thing to do."

"Leave him with me," said Emily quietly. "If he becomes worse, I will send for you."

"As you please, mum," said Balfour, with a heartless grin.

After he had left, Emily sat down on the floor beside Duke's low bed, which was a sort of imitation of a real bed, having four little legs to raise it off the floor and blankets and a pillow, and placed her cool hand on his hot, narrow head.

To date, Emily had been her own servant, tidying her own room and dressing herself. Now she seemed to have an embarrassment of servants, as the housekeeper and butler kept sending all sorts of delicacies up on trays. Nobody loved Duke, but they were impressed by Emily's "spunk" and by her quiet voice and general air of good breeding.

Emily had thought only of saving Duke's life. Her motives had been purely altruistic. Now she began to think

of herself. If Duke died, then she was sure she would be
turned out of doors.

She stared at the dog and fretted helplessly over him as
might an inexperienced mother over the sickness of her
first child.

And a fine mother I would make, thought Emily bitterly. But then I should not be in this coil. Provided I had
money enough, I should simply send for the physician.

The physician! Dr. Ackermann was due to call on Sir
Peregrine. Merciful heavens! It was past five o'clock and
the doctor might have left.

When the butler called once more to see if miss had
everything she needed for "the poor doggie," Emily begged
him to ask Dr. Ackermann to step along.

Fortunately for Emily, Sir Peregrine's doctor was of the
old-fashioned country variety and was not too high in the
instep to act as veterinarian when the occasion demanded.
He had a round cheerful face under a white tie wig and
wore a country-made snuff-colored coat with black waistcoat, short greenish drab trousers, and highblows—those
calf-length boots worn by countryfolk.

"Well, Miss . . . Winters, is it? Yes, yes. Now, let me
see the patient. Dear, dear."

His large, soft, white hands with their antique rings
prodded and poked and examined the recumbent Duke.

At last he went to his bag and produced a hornlike
instrument and a bottle of black liquid.

"Now, Miss Winters," said the doctor, "I want you to
hold the dog's head up . . . *right* up . . . so. Good. Now
if you will just open his mouth . . . th-a-a-t's right . . .
and pull his jaws apart." He inserted the horn, which
proved to be a kind of funnel, and poured the dose down
Duke's throat.

The dog opened its bleary eyes and whimpered faintly.

"That might do the trick," said Dr. Ackermann, getting

to his feet. "Keep him well wrapped up and away from drafts. I assume my bill will go to Sir Peregrine? Good, good."

He bustled out, leaving Emily alone with Duke.

And Emily, realizing she had done all she could possibly do to help the sick dog, felt suddenly bone-weary. She crawled on top of the bed, still in her clothes, and fell fast asleep.

She awoke some two hours later to find the fire had died down and the room was cold. Duke appeared to be in the throes of the nightmare of a lifetime.

Emily hurried out of bed and made up the fire and put fresh candles in the candlesticks, the old ones having burned down to the socket. And then she crouched down beside Duke and tried to shake him out of his nightmare. His eyes opened, red and staring, and then he began to vomit, great heaving retching bursts which seemed likely to tear him apart.

In desperation Emily rang the bell, and the servants, who were still enjoying the whole drama of the saving of Duke, arrived in droves.

Duke was tenderly lifted from his soiled bed like the most valued patient. Fresh linen was put on his bed, the mess was scrubbed up, and rose water was sprinkled about the room. At last, the dog's paroxysms subsided and he lay very still.

The servants stood around in silence as if at a wake. The rising storm howled in the chimney, and the candle flames danced, sending shadows flying up the faded wallpaper.

"Oh, *Duke*," said Emily tearfully, for she was quite sure he was dead.

And then Duke slowly opened his eyes and feebly wagged his silly plume of a tail from side to side.

What a cheer went up! The noise of rejoicing would

have given any sick human a relapse, but Duke bared his teeth in his travesty of a grin.

Footmen and housemaids hugged each other, cook put her head around the door promising nourishing broth and calves'-foot jelly, the butler suggested a little something to warm them all in the kitchen, and once again Emily was able to go to bed.

It was only when she was dropping off to sleep that she realized she had had no supper and was not in the least hungry, and that altruism has its uses. She had been so concerned about the welfare of the dog that she had not once thought of her own health. She had not even caught a chill.

The morning brought the return of sister Harriet and Clarissa Singleton from London.

Duke was stretched out in a deep sleep when Emily left him to visit Sir Peregrine, who, she convinced herself, must be anxious about the welfare of his dog.

Sir Peregrine, propped against his pillows, did vouchsafe a sort of apology at having left Emily in the lake with the dog. "Made me embarrassed, don't you see," he said. "Thought you was making a cake of yourself. But you're a brave girl, Emmy, and I won't forget it. I'm glad old Duke's going to pull through. He's had enough trials already."

"I never asked you where you found Duke," said Emily shyly.

"Found him over in Baxtead one market day. Local boys were torturing him something awful. He was nothing but skin and bone and damn near dead. Had had a bit too much to drink, so I thinks if I do something for this creature, the good Lord will take note of it in the hereafter. Don't like the animal much, and that's a fact. But I keep him as a sort of talisman. Only time in my life I did anything for anybody.''

''What about me?'' asked Emily. ''You took me out of the orphanage.''

''Oh, that,'' he said gruffly. ''Well, needed someone to look after Duke, don't you see. Nothing in that. In any case, it looks as if you won't be going over to Storm's place with us tonight. Better stay here and see Duke is fully well again. Could have a relapse when you're gone. Off you go now, and send Mrs. Singleton up to me.''

Emily did not want to see Clarissa, or Harriet, for that matter. She sent a footman with Sir Peregrine's message and then walked slowly along the corridor to her room.

So, she was not to go to Lord Storm's supper. Emily's eyes suddenly filled with tears, and she wearily wiped them away, thinking that the ordeal of yesterday must have enfeebled her more than she thought.

She naturally was not crying with disappointment. That idea was utterly ridiculous!

Chapter Three

Abbeywood Park, home of Lord Storm, had been made over to him on his twenty-fifth birthday by his father, the Earl of Freham, along with his father's junior title, Baron Storm. He rarely saw his parents, since they had frowned on the wild excesses of his youth, and although he had served his country bravely in the wars and had proved himself a good and sober landlord before that, they still shook their heads every time his name was mentioned and said that young Bart was sadly "rake-helly."

He had not meant to see any of the Manley Court menage again, but his old friend John Harris had come on a visit and had been so fascinated by Lord Storm's description of the household that he begged for a chance to see them all for himself.

And that was how the idea of the supper had come about.

Invitations had been sent not only to Manley Court but to various other county families. It was Lord Storm's thirty-third birthday, and he had a nagging feeling of guilt that his parents might expect to see him on that auspicious day, since they did not have much of a chance of seeing him at any other time.

But the invitations were out and the deed was done.

On the afternoon before the supper, Lord Storm and John Harris were sitting in the library, smoking, drinking, reading, and enjoying that splendid sort of bachelor existence that makes any right-minded female want to put a stop to it immediately.

"Still snowing, Bart," said John laconically. Both gentlemen were still attired in the dress they had worn for a morning's shooting, which is about the nearest a gentleman ever gets to fancy dress—indulging himself by wearing the brightest of jackets, the oldest of breeches, and then sinking his feet into the comfort of a pair of old-fashioned round-toed Hessians.

Lord Storm was dressed in a long sky-blue plush jacket, and John Harris sported a pea-green affair with a great deal of pockets all about it.

Lord Storm glanced toward the window but did not bother to reply to his friend's remark about the snow.

Of course, thought his lordship, pretending to read, perhaps it would be better if it snowed so much that nobody could come. But that would be a pity, for his chef and his kitchen staff had worked long and hard on the buffet supper, and the orchestra he had hired for the occasion were fiddling away somewhere in the back regions of the house.

Besides, it would only be doing that pert Miss Winters a kindness to show her that he had no dishonorable intentions toward her at all. He must have a guilty conscience about his behavior, or why else had he thought of her almost constantly? He could not be in love. That idea was laughable. A gentleman did not fall in love with anyone below his station . . . not enough to marry, anyway.

What was John saying? Something about never having seen such a change in anyone?

"Who are you talking about?" asked Lord Storm, putting down his newspaper.

"Why, you," said John. "I was sitting here thinking over old times and how wild we used to be. And now look at us. Two staid gentlemen beside the library fire.

"I mean, you never laugh much now, Bart, do you? I mean, I *know* you, but you must seem like a very high and mighty gentleman to those that don't."

"I don't find much to laugh about," said Lord Storm. "And don't remind me of the follies of my youth. I find a rather glacial manner an advantage, John. It keeps the mushrooms and matching mamas at bay, not to mention their silly daughters. Now come, John! In all honesty, has any female ever made you laugh?"

"Old Dottie down at the Pig and Whistle in Streatham," replied John promptly.

"I am not talking about barmaids with generous appurtenances and a native wit. I am talking about ladies."

"Oh, them. Well, now you come to mention it, no. But who wants to laugh at 'em? I like being surrounded by soft young things with round white arms and neat ankles."

"Pah!" said Lord Storm. "If that's all you want, get yourself an opera dancer. You don't need to marry them or do the pretty by them."

"Haven't you ever been in love, Bart?"

"No," said Lord Storm with unnecessary vehemence, sending a sudden vision of a log and a girl and a dog and a warm, fresh pair of trembling lips whirling off to a dark corner of his mind.

"Be careful, then. You're at a dangerous age. You said one of the Manley Court lot was a dasher."

"Yes, a Mrs. Singleton. Very beautiful."

"And what of the girl you mentioned? The Cinderella of Manley Court who sits guarding some dreadful incontinent mongrel and waiting for Prince Charming with the slipper of glass?"

"Oh, nothing out of the common way," said Lord Storm carelessly. "One of those meek little household martyrs who can never stand up for themselves. She is a fairly pretty sort of poor relation, destined to turn into an old spinsterish poor relation."

"And the two Miss Kiplings?"

"I shall not trouble myself to describe them, since they are no longer in residence at Manley Court."

"Any other charmers?"

"Not from Manley Court. Phyllis Whitaker is charming but married, as is Felicity Manners."

"Well, you ain't going to fall in love this evening," said John cheerfully. "Oh, look! It's stopped snowing at last."

Lord Storm began to find himself looking forward to the evening with uncharacteristic enthusiasm as the hour approached for the guests to arrive.

He had dressed with unusual care, fussing to make sure his valet had stretched his evening coat across his broad shoulders so that there should be no suggestion of a wrinkle. His evening trousers were molded to his long muscular legs like a pair of ballet tights, and his green-and-gold-striped stockings were fitted into dancing pumps of the finest leather. He picked up his silver-backed brushes and attacked his hair till it shone like white gold.

The supper was laid out in one of a chain of saloons which ran the length of the first floor. He would receive his guests on the landing. Dancing was to be held in the Red Saloon, which was large enough to accommodate at least thirty couples. Food was to be served in the Blue

Saloon and cards to be played in the Yellow. Abbeywood
Park had been built some hundred years before, and then
the decoration of the saloons had matched their name. But
with the passing of years, the colors had changed. The Red
Saloon was now blue; the Blue was Egyptian black and
gold. But they still retained their original names.

He was in a position at the top of the stairs as the first
carriages arrived.

Mrs. Whitaker and Mrs. Manners and their husbands
were the first to arrive. Then came the lord lieutenant of
the county, Sir Gerald Baron, with his wife and two
daughters, and then the Marquess of Dunster with his two
sons.

Finally, from his station at the top of the stairs, he saw
the party from Manley Court arriving. James Manley had
cast his clericals and was wearing a very dandified bottle-
green silk jacket with tails to his ankles, knee breeches
with great bunches of colored ribbons, and a striped waistcoat which boasted a great quantity of fobs and seals. He
had powdered his hair with flour, not wanting to pay the
iniquitous tax on hair powder.

Clarissa was there, looking quite dazzling in jonquil
sarsenet, and Harriet, as imposing as any dowager in a
formidable turban and gown, both of purple velvet. In
fact, thought Lord Storm, she looked just like an illustra-
tion of Hamlet's aunt.

Sir Peregrine was extremely fine in a silk coat of old-
fashioned cut, Cadogan wig, and knee breeches. He was in
the throes of one of his deaf spells, so all present obligingly
cranked their voices up a few notches, although most of
them had very loud voices to begin with. After all, most of
the gentlemen one met were slightly if not totally deaf
from their addiction to shooting anything that moved on
their estates—except the fox; heaven forbid!—and so one
had to cultivate a very loud voice indeed. Those who

uncharitably thought that the overbearing, loud, damn-you-to-hell voices of the English aristocracy came from arrogance and insensitivity were wrong; they came from necessity.

And so Lord Storm found himself demanding in a voice to make the welkin ring, "Dear me! Where is Miss Winters? Not indisposed, I trust?"

"What?" wheezed Sir Peregrine as he advanced toward the Red Saloon, swinging one gouty foot in front of him. "No, no, no. Duke's ill. Stayed back to care for him, don't you see."

Lord Storm was aware of his friend John's bright eyes on his face, and felt he somehow could not pursue the subject of Miss Winters any further.

Clarissa fastened her luminous gaze on John Harris. She felt she had failed to attract Lord Storm, and she had never been the kind of lady to waste her time on lost causes. Mr. Harris was as tall as Lord Storm, with a pleasant, square face and merry brown eyes. He looked infinitely more approachable. It was rumored he was worth twenty thousand a year.

Footmen passed among the company with drinks, negus and ratafia for the ladies and punch, champagne, or hock for the men.

Mrs. Tommy Whitaker and Mrs. Harry Manners were young county ladies of no particular looks. They were, on the other hand, thoroughly pleasant and devoted to their respective husbands. Tommy Whitaker and Harry Manners had known Lord Storm before he went to the wars and were on easy terms with him.

Lord Storm stood talking to them of this and that, all the social chitchat of the district, and all the while his mind wondered why on earth Emily had not come. Surely the servants could have looked after a mere dog! And since she was such a favorite with Sir Peregrine, surely she could have coaxed him into letting her come.

But to ask Sir Peregrine for further intelligence meant shouting in his ear, and that way Lord Storm would have to broadcast his interest in Emily to the whole room. When he had finished talking to the Mannerses and the Whitakers, he edged across the room to where the Reverend James Manley was standing by the fireplace, gazing into the flames with a singularly nasty look on his thin, wrinkled face as if the branches of apple wood were so many sinners being slowly consumed in hellfire.

Lord Storm politely asked James about various parish matters and then asked abruptly, "Why did Miss Winters not come?"

"She is employed by my brother to care for his abominable pet," fluted James in a voice that carried to every corner of the Red Saloon, "so no doubt that is what she is doing now."

Mr. John Harris glanced across the room at his friend in dawning surprise. Lord Storm was certainly showing a great deal of interest in a girl he had damned as a "meek household martyr."

Harriet came forward and joined James, her purple turban with its osprey plumes nodding vigorously. "I hear you are talking about Miss Winters," she said. "The girl has no breeding at all. So hurly-burly. The wretched dog was nearly drowned in the lake, and would have been too, had not that silly girl decided to enact some Haymarket scene by plunging in to rescue the animal. It would have died and saved us all a great deal of trouble, but Miss Winters decided to call in Sir Peregrine's physician to attend to the beast. Such impudence!"

"I trust Miss Winters came to no harm?" said Lord Storm.

"Not she," sniffed Harriet ungraciously. "Strong as an ox."

As the musicians played the first bars of the opening country dance, Lord Storm resolutely banished the thought of Emily from his mind. He was a punctilious host and he set himself to please. Mrs. Singleton quite worked herself into his good graces at supper by remarking it was a pity Emily was not present, since she did not seem to have much in the way of fun and parties. Normally shrewd, Lord Storm failed to realize that the clever Clarissa had judged his interest in Emily to a nicety and planned to make full use of it. Certainly Mr. Harris appeared to have fallen under her spell, but she wanted to have one more try at engaging Lord Storm's interest before she gave up her pursuit in that direction. She had not enjoyed her loss of social status through being married to a City merchant and was determined, if possible, to marry a title next. Mr. Harris was, however, from the untitled aristocracy, and perhaps he might have to do.

At last the evening was over, and John Harris and Lord Storm sat over the brandy decanter before retiring.

"What a rum lot they were," said John. "I mean the lot from Manley Court—with the exception of Mrs. Singleton, of course.

"I can't help wondering why you asked them. Sir Peregrine is an awful old bore, Miss Manley is a sour old spinster, and Mr. James Manley is quite mad. Of course," went on John slyly, "perhaps the fair Miss Winters would have brightened the party?"

"Perhaps," said Lord Storm with seeming indifference. "I was merely returning hospitality. I should not have inflicted them on my other guests. But it's over and I need never see any of them again. And, by the way, I would like to remind you that *you* were the one who begged to have a look at them."

"Aren't you going to call in person tomorrow?" asked John curiously. It was the custom to call on the ladies one had danced with the night before. Of course, one could send one's servant.

"I might," said his lordship. "Or I might ask you to carry my compliments. *You*, no doubt, are panting to call on Mrs. Singleton."

"As the hart panteth after the water brooks," said John, grinning.

"I don't know if I shall accompany you," said Lord Storm. "Probably not."

But somehow John was not surprised when Lord Storm volunteered to go with him the following day.

A bitter wind from the east threatened more snow as they drove slowly and carefully in the direction of Manley Court. Despite his many-caped greatcoat, John shivered on the box. "Why don't you let your coachman drive?" he complained. "We could then be sitting inside where we belong, wrapped in bear rugs and with a few hot bricks at our feet."

"I like driving," said Lord Storm, feathering the Manley Court gatepost to an inch to illustrate his point. His carriage swung up the long drive to Manley Park, but John noticed that as they approached the house, Lord Storm slowed his team and his eyes raked over the lawns as if looking for someone.

Miss Harriet Manley was glad to see them in a sour kind of a way but reported that Sir Peregrine had taken one of his turns and was keeping to his bedchamber.

James Manley was for once about his parish business, although he usually left that side of affairs to his over-worked curate.

John Harris sat down on a sofa beside Mrs. Singleton

and kept one ear cocked to see if his friend would ask for
the mysterious Miss Winters.

But Lord Storm did not. Very soon the stipulated ten
minutes for making a call were over, and both gentlemen
arose to their feet, Mr. Harris having begged permission to
take Mrs. Singleton riding the next day and having been
accepted.

They said goodbye to the ladies and collected their coats
and hats and gloves in the hall.

The butler, Rogers, was holding open the door when
Lord Storm heard a little rumbling sound from abovestairs,
the scampering of paws, and a ripple of enchanting laughter.

"Miss Winters is at home?" he asked the butler.

"Yes, my lord. The weather being inclement, Miss
Winters is exercising the master's dog in the long gallery."

Lord Storm stood for a few moments frowning at the
floor while the butler waited patiently as a cold wind
whipped across the hall.

"Present my compliments to Miss Winters," said his
lordship at last, "and ask her if she could spare me a few
moments."

The butler inclined his head and went off to deliver the
message.

"Wait for me in the carriage, John," said Lord Storm.
"I shall not be above a few minutes."

"Oh, no, you don't," said John cheerfully. "Am I not
to have a look at this meek household martyr?"

"No," said Lord Storm bleakly. "Be a good chap,
John, and do as I say. I do not feel like explaining
myself."

"Oh, very well. But I'll wait *inside* the carriage, and
you may freeze on the box on the return journey."

Rogers soon returned to say that Miss Winters was
prepared to see his lordship.

Lord Storm mounted the stairs after the butler, wondering what he should say and why he was making such an effort to see the girl anyway. Before he reached the doors of the long gallery, he decided it was because he felt in need of apologizing to her for his cavalier behavior. Once that distasteful task was over, then he could forget her.

Rogers threw open the doors of the long gallery.

"Lord Storm," he announced, and then retired, leaving the doors punctiliously open, since Miss Winters was not chaperoned.

Emily turned a flushed face to his. "I shall just roll this ball once more for Duke." She rolled a wooden croquet ball along the polished length of the gallery, and Duke went bounding after it. Having seized the ball in his jaws, he stood staring wildly about him, then dropped it at his feet, keeled over with a thump, and went promptly to sleep.

"Poor old Duke," said Emily. "He is still exhausted after his ordeal, my lord. He nearly drowned. I have been trying to teach him to retrieve, but he does not really like to fetch anything other than a stick."

"The animal is utterly hopeless," Lord Storm smiled. "He's also much too fat. His back's like that of a well-fed sheep."

Now, Emily had not become any more fond of Duke with the passing of the winter days, but to her surprise she found herself resenting Lord Storm's criticism of the animal immensely. Duke looked vulnerable and ugly, lying stretched out, chasing rabbits in his sleep.

"It's not his fault," said Emily hotly. "He's never been trained to anything. You are too harsh—on people and on animals."

Lord Storm's lips tightened. He was not used to being criticized. In fact, he could not remember anyone's having even dared to do so, with the exception of his parents and John Harris.

Then he recollected his apology.

"Pray sit down, Miss Winters. There is something I wish to say to you."

Emily dutifully sat down in a hard chair near one of the long windows which lined one wall of the gallery. Lord Storm stood in front of the empty fireplace.

Emily was wearing the plaid gown which Mrs. Otley had given her. Her black hair gleamed with health, and her blue eyes surveyed him curiously.

"Miss Winters," began Lord Storm, "I wish to make you an apology. I am not in the way of thrusting myself on young ladies of good breeding. . . ."

"I see." Emily smiled. "You usually confine your attentions to ladies of bad breeding."

"No. Let me finish, miss," said Lord Storm furiously. "I am making you a humble apology, dammit, and the least you can do is sit there quietly until I am finished."

"Yes, my lord," said Emily meekly, although her eyes were dancing.

"As I was saying," went on his lordship, beginning to stride up and down, "I am very sorry if I caused you any embarrassment. There!"

"Thank you," said Emily demurely. "But what made you think I would welcome your attentions?"

Lord Storm flushed. "I assumed, madam, that you were waiting there to waylay me. It has happened before. I mean, in similar circumstances."

"What a *very* lucky man you are, to be sure," said Emily. "All these fair damsels throwing themselves at you."

He stared at her haughtily, and then all at once burst out laughing.

"You wicked girl," he said. "How dare you tease me so, and what a coxcomb you make me look! I am not so vain, you know. It is not my face or figure that the fair sex pursue, but my title and my fortune.''

"Alas! Poor Lord Storm. But it is so very tempting, you know. I mean your fortune, rather than your title. Still, I do not think I could ever be so mercenary,'' said Emily candidly. "Of course, I *might* be in danger of thinking myself *into* love with some gentleman in order to secure myself a home.''

He walked toward her, pulled forward a chair, and sat down opposite so that their knees were almost touching. All at once, Emily felt uneasy. At close quarters, she was only too aware of a sort of emanation of virility coming from him. "Your position here is not a happy one,'' he said, forcing his eyes not to stray to her mouth, which looked so very soft and yielding.

"It is far better than the orphanage,'' said Emily candidly. "They were not cruel to me there, but it was so very cold in winter and there was never enough to eat. It is the insecurity that frightens me. I don't know who this mysterious Manley relative is who paid for my keep in the orphanage or whether he—or she—will support me should Sir Peregrine die. Miss Manley has made it plain that neither I nor Duke can depend on house room.''

"I have business in town, sometime in the coming weeks,'' he said slowly. "Perhaps I could call on your lawyers and explain your predicament. Do you know their names and direction?''

"Yes, my lord. Summers and Summers of Lincoln's Inn Fields.''

"Very well, I will see what I can do.''

"Oh, thank you,'' said Emily, deciding that Lord Storm was really quite human after all.

"Perhaps you would care to come driving with me tomorrow?'' he said, smiling into her eyes in a way that made her knees turn to jelly.

"Oh, my lord, I would like that above all things, but it cannot be so. I am not permitted to leave Duke. Sir Peregrine has the idea that either Miss Manley or Mr. Manley will poison him."

"That is utterly ridiculous! But by all means let us humor the old man. We will take that wretched animal driving as well."

"Oh, *thank* you, my lord!" cried Emily, quite pink with excitement. "I did so want to go to your party," she added shyly after a moment. "But Duke was so very ill, although as you can see, he has rallied amazingly."

Duke opened one beady eye and stared at Lord Storm, gave a cavernous yawn, and went back to sleep.

"I gather you showed exceptional bravery in rescuing the animal," said Lord Storm, rising to his feet, while Emily blushed and disclaimed.

He took her hand in his. "Until tomorrow, Miss Winters," he said, dropping a light kiss on her hand.

"Unless it snows too much, my lord," said Emily, anxiously looking out of the nearest window.

"I am sure nature will favor us." He smiled on her again and took his leave.

Emily sat down suddenly again and hugged her middle.

"Oh, let it not snow," she whispered to the sleeping dog. "I would love to see something of the countryside, and I am so tired of being cooped up in here." And she would not admit that her intense anticipation was for any further reason.

The weather strained Emily's nerves to the limit. First it snowed, then it rained, then it froze, then it thawed, and then it froze and snowed again—just one of the many reasons why the English weather keeps the English people in a perpetual state of outrage.

But by the next afternoon a little yellow winter sun

shone dimly through a haze of thin gray cloud and icicles glittered everywhere, hanging in long gleaming stalactites from the eaves. The day was hushed and silent, as only the countryside can be in the chill grip of winter.

Emily was trembling with excitement. She had fought against the temptation to write to her friends at the orphanage to tell them she was going out driving with a lord, telling herself sternly that in the first place, they might not believe her, and in the second, if they did it might make them discontented. She had been further cheered by Mrs. Singleton's sudden friendliness, and by the present from Mrs. Otley, the housekeeper, of a smart carriage dress in red merino with a warm pelisse to match.

Mrs. Otley had confided that the Kipling girls had left a whole wardrobe behind, something that they usually did after their visits, so that their parents would furnish them with a new one.

Mrs. Singleton had left at two o'clock with John Harris. Emily waited in her room, her hand on Duke's smooth head. The dog, sensing her agitation, sat very still, staring up at her in an unnerving way out of his close-set eyes. She had brushed his rough shaggy coat until it shone like black-and-gold lacquer.

"He didn't say what time he would call," murmured Emily. "It is a good thing Harriet has gone to the rectory, for she would not approve at all. Oh, pray let Sir Peregrine keep to his room. He might stop me going. Oh, what if he does not come!"

But at precisely quarter to three, an excited housemaid popped her head around the door to announce that Lord Storm had called to take miss driving.

Emily went downstairs, forcing herself not to run.

Duke, on seeing Lord Storm and sensing his mistress's delight and resenting it, promptly sat down in the hall and refused to budge.

"*Do* come along, Duke," begged Emily. "Oh, he *must* come, my lord, or I cannot leave."

She pulled Duke by the collar. His rump slid a little way along the polished floor of the hall, but he bumped against an island of Persian carpet and dug in all four paws.

"Oh, *Duke*," said Emily despairingly.

Lord Storm looked at Emily's distressed face. He gazed down at Duke, who scowled up at him in a belligerent way.

"Come!" Lord Storm held out his arm to Emily.

"I can't!" she wailed.

Lord Storm rapped his short riding crop against his boot and said softly to Duke, "To heel!" Then he turned and marched to the door without looking behind him. At a signal from the butler, who had been an anxious spectator, two burly footmen ran forward, seized Duke, and carried him out quietly behind Lord Storm and deposited him beside the carriage.

"There you are," said his lordship when he turned around and saw Duke. "All you need to do is give the proper command."

Emily, who had followed the footmen out, stifled a wild giggle. Lord Storm was completely unaware that Duke had had to be carried out bodily.

Emily was helped up to the box, and the two footmen lifted Duke up by the scruff of the neck and threw him up to her. The dog looked remarkably like a sulky child. He crouched on the box next to Emily, his eyes darting from side to side the way they did when he was plotting mischief.

And so they set off, with Duke riding bodkin between Emily and Lord Storm, his narrow head twisting alternately to look up into one face and then the other.

They drove silently through the glittering world of ice, the horses' hooves muffled by the powdery snow. Then

Lord Storm began to describe the various landmarks of the district.

The folly on the hill had been built by Sir Peregrine's father, the church at Baxtead was supposed to be Saxon, and there was to be a skating party near the town of Rumford some fifteen miles distant.

Emily tucked a fold of a carriage rug around Duke's back and enjoyed herself as much as any seventeen-year-old miss would when attired in a new dress, or one new at least to her, and escorted by a handsome lord. She was mature enough to know that she was dazzled by Lord Storm's title and had enough common sense to enjoy it all without indulging in self-recrimination or guilt.

He began to ask her questions about the orphanage and how long she had been there. Emily told him that she could not remember ever having been anywhere else. He listened as she warmed to her subject, telling of the party that a certain charitable lady had once given for them and how they had been whipped when it was discovered that she and some of the other girls had stolen cakes to hide in their dormitory; of winter days breaking ice in the wash-basins; of the endless diet of gruel and burned porridge; and of the day-in-and-day-out sermons urging them to be grateful and pray for their benefactors.

"Of course, I could never really pray properly for mine," said Emily anxiously. "You see, I didn't know who he or she was. And then nothing seemed to have been planned for my future. Seventeen is quite old to be still at the orphanage. I had already begun to instruct some of the younger girls, and the teachers said I was coming along nicely, so perhaps I might ask them to take me back. But poor Duke! Who will want him?"

"A dog, like a man," said Lord Storm, "should be trained to some occupation. If I lost my money, I could at least return to the army."

"But not as an officer," pointed out Emily. "You do not realize how much money does for you, because you have always had it."

Lord Storm tried to think of some way to argue this point, decided he could not, and returned to the subject of Duke.

"The animal has been dreadfully spoiled. He could perhaps be trained as a gun dog, but he has a mean face and no doubt would eat the birds."

"That is not his fault," said Emily. "Sir Peregrine rescued him when some boys were torturing him to death. He has not always been spoiled."

"I am surprised to hear Sir Peregrine has some altruistic feelings. I would have credited him with none at all. Has he made no provision for you in his will?"

"Oh, no! Nor should I expect such a thing! He made me understand that my sole function and reason for being allowed to stay at Manley Court was to take care of Duke. Duke is a sort of talisman, you see. Besides, he has so many close relatives."

"All of Sir Peregrine's relatives—and that includes his brother and sister—are well-to-do. They have no need of his fortune. I think the problem is that the bulk of Sir Peregrine's fortune is in diamonds, and that somehow excites their greed."

"Well, it does not excite mine," said Emily. "All I want is one small place to call my own. Perhaps have a few little things of my own, a few books and pictures."

"You are well-looking in your way," said Lord Storm, leaning down at the Baxtead toll and flipping a shilling to the gatekeeper. "You will no doubt marry."

"How?" asked Emily with interest. "I thought marriage was a matter of having parents and being presented."

"Yes, yes. But surely we are assuming the worst. Miss

Manley may be shrewish, but she will not turn you out of doors.''

''Oh, yes, she will,'' said Emily with conviction. ''She said so.''

''Well, then, James Manley. Surely he will consider it his Christian duty to care for you.''

''Not he,'' said Emily. ''According to Mr. Manley, I am a viper being nourished in the Manley bosom. He firmly believes my place is in either the orphanage or the workhouse and it has been flying in the face of Providence to keep me from my natural lot.''

Lord Storm decided to change the subject. He could not quite believe the Manley family as black as Emily painted them. One often said things one did not mean. It was inconceivable that the Manleys would put her out of doors as soon as Sir Peregrine died.

He reined in his horses and pointed with his whip. ''Look! The waterfall over there is quite frozen.''

Emily stared in delight. The sun, now low on the horizon, had changed to red, and the icy spikes of the petrified waterfall shone crimson.

If only this moment could stay frozen in time, thought Emily suddenly. But he was urging the horses forward again at a smart pace, and Emily swallowed a lump of disappointment that her treat was so soon to be over.

But he surprised her by saying, ''I am taking you to my home for tea. My housekeeper will be chaperon enough, I assure you. It is no use, I suppose, suggesting that this dog be put in the stables?''

''No . . . please,'' said Emily. ''He is still not very strong.''

Emily studied Lord Storm's home with interest as the carriage approached it up a long drive. It had two projecting wings on either side of the main building, rather like an E with the center stroke knocked out.

Emily found herself becoming nervous at the idea of being alone with him. What if he renewed his attentions?

But a very motherly housekeeper was on hand to greet them, and the drawing room into which she ushered them had such a cheerful fire and such pretty pictures and china that Emily quite forgot her fears and happily surrendered her pelisse and bonnet.

A table was set before the fire, with a small sofa drawn up before it. Emily sat down on the sofa, Lord Storm sat down beside her, and Duke jumped up and squeezed himself in between them, grinning up at Lord Storm in a highly irritating way.

"Down! Get down this minute!" snapped Lord Storm.

Emily fumbled in her pocket and surreptitiously drew out a sugar loaf and threw it across the carpet. Duke leaped down after it.

"There you are," said his lordship. "A bit of discipline is all that animal needs."

Fortunately for Emily, Duke, after eating the sugar loaf, decided to go to sleep on the carpet. Had he not been so tired, she knew he would have tried to push himself onto the sofa again.

Emily found herself wondering what it would be like to be brought up to all this ease and comfort and simply take it for granted. But it seemed as if Lord Storm did not quite accept it all completely without thought.

He began to talk about his estates, saying there was a great deal of work to be done on them. "Things were not managed properly in my absence," he said. "There have been bad harvests, and that means hardship. A good landlord should not collect rents after a bad harvest. If the tenants and tenant farmers are well fed and well housed, then the estate runs like clockwork, bad year or no.

"If you take all the money out of the land and have badly housed tenants and starving workers, then you have insurrections—and who shall blame them? In a strange way, I might have been better employed staying here, instead of fighting for my country. I am a good farmer but an indifferent soldier. I think my heart was never really set on a military career, but I felt I had to do my bit to stop Napolean's march across Europe."

"You were wounded?" said Emily gently.

"Yes, my leg. That healed all right, but I was weak with fever and nigh delirious for a month. I was in a sort of makeshift hospital in Lisbon for most of my illness, so by the time I sailed for home, I swear I was nearly recovered.

"But I have been told it was a near thing. I know at one point I was near death. In the stifling heat of that so-called hospital, I began to realize what I had nearly lost. My tenants and servants were glad to see me back instead of cursing me for an absentee landlord. The least I can do is see the land in good heart before I leave again . . . if I leave. Ah, here comes Mr. Harris."

John Harris made his bow to Emily and accepted a cup of tea, taking a chair by the fire and stretching his boots out to the blaze.

"It's snowing again." He yawned. "I have just taken Mrs. Singleton home, and there's a great deal of commotion at Manley Court. Sir Peregrine's lawyer, Mr. Summers, has arrived from London and is closeted with him. Sir Peregrine's physician is there too and fears the old man will not last the night."

Emily sprang to her feet. "I must go," she said in great agitation.

"Of course." Lord Storm had risen with her. "I'll drive you home immediately. I realize it is not proper for you to be alone in a closed carriage with me, Miss Winters, and we certainly cannot travel on the box now it is snowing. I will get one of the housemaids to accompany us.''

Despite her agitation, Emily was relieved that he was determined to honor the conventions.

The snow was falling very hard indeed when they arrived at Manley Court.

Rogers, the butler, met them at the door with gloomy tidings. Sir Peregrine Manley was dead.

As he was speaking, the door of the drawing room opened and Harriet came hurrying out. She did not notice Lord Storm, for her eyes were fixed on Emily and Duke.

''My brother's dead,'' she said coldly. ''So you, Miss Winters, can leave right now and take that cur with you.''

Duke let out a low growl and began to advance on Harriet, who let out a scream, fled back into the drawing room, and slammed the door.

Emily stood very still and white-faced. Then she seemed to summon up her courage. ''I do not wish to be a burden on you, my lord, but I would deem it a great favor if you could manage to convey me back to the orphanage.''

Lord Storm stood looking at her. His brain raced. He could not offer her anything less than marriage, for that would be taking ungentlemanly advantage of her distress. But he could not ask her to marry him. *He could not.* His pride in his name would not allow him to offer marriage to a girl of such doubtful family history.

''Very well,'' he said quietly.

Behind him, Rogers let out a little sigh, almost of disappointment.

''Come, Duke,'' said Emily in a choked little voice. ''I have only a few belongings, my lord. I shall not keep you waiting long.''

Lord Storm nodded, his eyes hooded and enigmatic.

* * *

Emily stood helplessly in her room. Word of her departure spread quickly through the house. Mrs. Otley arrived with a pair of housemaids, and together they began to pack Emily's belongings.

"You must brace up, ma'am," said Mrs. Otley. "It's downright wicked of Miss Manley, though it's not my place to question my betters."

When everything was ready, Mrs. Otley summoned a footman to carry Emily's trunk down to the hall.

"Leave me a few moments, Mrs. Otley," said Emily. "I want to be alone, just for a moment."

The housekeeper curtsied and left.

Emily pulled a chair up to the window and sat down, looking around the room, suddenly overcome by such a burst of fury and rage she thought she would be ill. How callous and unfeeling were the Manleys! How easily they took all this for granted! Her eyes roamed from the fire crackling on the hearth to the sofa, comfortable bed, and rich hangings. Heat and food and warmth. Never to be hers again. For one glorious afternoon she had been treated as a young lady of quality. Now she belonged nowhere.

Duke pushed his head against her hand, and she absentmindedly scratched his ears. "I'll beg them at the orphanage to let me keep you, Duke. But I don't think they will. Oh, Duke. What is to become of us?"

At last she arose and, taking a last look around, went slowly from the room.

Lord Storm was standing in the hall when she descended the stairs, talking to an elderly gentleman. He broke off as Emily approached.

"It seems, Miss Winters, that we are to stay for the reading of the will. Sir Peregrine's dying wish was that you should be present. To my surprise he has named me executor. Allow me to present Mr. Summers to you. Mr. Summers, Miss Winters.''

The lawyer peered shortsightedly at Emily over a pair of gold-rimmed pince-nez. "Ah, Miss Winters! Delighted!''

"Oh, Mr. Summers,'' cried Emily. "You must help me. Please tell me the name of my benefactor, the person who paid for my keep at the orphanage. And I have longed to know the names of my parents.''

Mr. Summers looked uncomfortable. "I am afraid I must respect Sir Peregrine's wishes and wait until the will is read before the family.

"It concerns yourself, Miss Winters, and Mr. and Miss Manley. Since we are all present, it would be an idea to gather in the library. I have already informed Mr. and Miss Manley of my intention, and they await us there.''

Wonderingly, Emily followed the lawyer and Lord Storm. Duke padded in the shadow of her skirts. It had finally penetrated his small brain that things were in a miserable way and somehow that state of affairs was shortly to affect his comfort.

The library was a great cavernous room, little used by the family. Harriet and James were sitting on chairs before the table. Mr. Summers went immediately to the table and sat at a chair behind it. Lord Storm stood by the fireplace, and Emily drew up a chair near the table. All eyes were on the lawyer.

"Now that we are all gathered,'' began the lawyer, crackling open sheets of parchment, "I shall communicate the contents of Sir Peregrine Manley's will as briefly as possible. May I suggest the ladies have their vinaigrettes handy? They may find the intelligence contained herein of a somewhat shocking nature.''

"Do simply go ahead,'' snapped Harriet.

The lawyer looked at Lord Storm, who nodded.

In his dry, precise voice, he began:

" 'Miss Emily Winters is my natural daughter, fathered by me on a serving wench at the Pelican Inn in Bristol by the name of Jessie Winters, now dead many years—' "

"Aha!" cried Harriet. "I knew there was bad blood there!"

"Really, madam," said the little lawyer coldly. "I think Miss Winters has received enough of a shock without having to suffer further unnecessary cruelty. I wished to impart the news to her in private, but it was Sir Peregrine's dying wish that the news be given to her thus."

The door opened and Clarissa Singleton floated in, smiling brightly. Her maid had informed her of the reading of the will. Her curious eyes roved from Harriet's bright malicious eyes, to James Manley's glassy stare, to Lord Storm's rigid face, to Emily's white shocked one.

"Have I missed anything?" she asked.

Mr. Summers ignored her. "I will now proceed with the will. Before I begin I can assure you that Sir Peregrine Manley was of sound mind. This is a summary of what provision he has made.

"To Miss Winters, Sir Peregrine has left Manley Court, his estates and all other properties, and the income therefrom. Miss Manley and Mr. James Manley may reside at Manley Court subject to Miss Winters's permission."

Harriet ran her tongue across her dry lips. James turned a dull purple. "The diamonds," he spluttered. "What of the diamonds?"

"I will read what Sir Peregrine has written," said Mr. Summers, settling his pince-nez and peering at the paper with maddening deliberation.

" 'My fortune in diamonds, with the exception of the Manley diamond collar, which goes to Miss Emily Winters, I leave to—' "

"Yes. *Yes!*" said Harriet, her face thrust forward like a gargoyle.

" 'I leave to my dog Duke.' "

"What?" cried everyone in the room.

" 'On Duke's death,' " continued Mr. Summers, " 'the diamonds will be divided equally among the following: my sister, Harriet; my brother, James; my cousin, Mrs. Clarissa Singleton; and my nieces, Fanny and Betty Kipling.' And now, Miss Winters, I have the Manley collar here.'' He opened a black box and threw back the lid. The heavy collar of diamonds flashed fire in the candlelight. Mr. Summers stood up and held it out to Emily.

Like a sleepwalker, she moved forward and took the collar and stared down at it.

Then she turned and looked around the room.

Duke was sitting up in an armchair by the fire, his head cocked to one side, watching the proceedings.

Emily walked forward and fastened the collar of diamonds around the dog's neck and then stood with her hand on his head.

She gave a harsh, ugly laugh. "Look well on us," she said. "The mongrels have the diamonds!"

Duke lifted his black lips in a long slow grin while the diamonds blazed and flashed among the shaggy gold-and-black fur at his neck.

It was just about then that Harriet Manley began to scream. . . .

Chapter Four

Two days after the reading of the will, Miss Emily Winters was sitting in the drawing room before the fire, hemming handkerchiefs, while a blizzard raged outside.

On the other side of the fire, Lord Storm sat reading a five-day-old newspaper. He had been unable to return to his home because of the snow, and so he had been put under a sort of house arrest, confined with a girl he would now like to avoid.

Lord Storm was very much a product of his class and upbringing. Illegitimate girls with serving maid mothers were promptly classed as "persons" in his mind. He now viewed Emily through this distorting glass, and, had it not been for the snow, he might have gone out of his way not to see her again. He was, however, a well-meaning man and was unfailingly polite to Emily, and would have been quite shocked had he known that she recognized the change in him and knew the reason for it.

Emily had wept long and hard after the reading of the

will—that is, as soon as she managed to escape to the privacy of her bedchamber. She did not want to think of the selfish Sir Peregrine as her father, and she could not mourn the mother she had never known.

She had barely seen Harriet or James or Clarissa since the reading of the will. The ladies had mostly kept to their rooms, and James had fled to the rectory directly he had heard the bad news and could not return because of the snow.

And so she and Lord Storm had been left much in each other's company. Emily knew he would never make advances to her again. That sensuous, brooding look in his hooded gray eyes had disappeared, replaced by a cool clear disinterested gaze. Now that he was indifferent to her, she found to her horror that she could not now look at him without remembering the feel of his lips on hers and the hard, firm feel of his hands on her body. She bitterly put it down to lustful thoughts engendered by her low origins.

She covertly studied the hard, tanned planes of his face, the square chin, and long mouth, all under the shadow of the two wings of white-blond hair which sprang from his forehead. His hands holding the newspaper were strong, with long fingers and polished nails. At that moment, he raised his eyes, and she felt herself blushing and looked around for Duke.

"He is snoring over on that sofa—that is, if you are looking for that cursed spoiled mongrel," he said. "Have you considered, Miss Winters, that the dog's life is now very much in danger? That that reprehensible carriage rug over there stands between five people and a fortune in diamonds?"

"I hadn't thought . . ." said Emily, plucking nervously at the material of her gown:

"And what do you intend to do with Manley Court?"

Emily looked at him wide-eyed. "Sell it, I suppose," she faltered.

His lips folded in a grim line. "Just as one might have expected," he remarked, picking up his newspaper again.

"And *why* is that just what one might have expected?" demanded Emily sharply. "And furthermore, my lord, you are reading that newspaper upside down!"

He threw the newspaper away with a dramatic gesture which was spoiled by the newspaper's landing in the fire. He had to leap to his feet and pick up the flaming paper with the tongs and stuff it down under the logs so that it would not fly up the chimney and set it on fire.

"There are a great number of people, Miss Winters," he said glacially, "who have served Manley Court for many years, and their fathers and mothers before them. Think of Mrs. Otley and Rogers."

Emily flushed. "I didn't think," she said, "and I'm not to be blamed for that. I know nothing of the running of an estate."

"You have a steward—Mr. Hardy—and Mrs. Otley and Rogers run the house."

"And what do I do with the terrible Miss Manley?"

"You can simply order her to leave. Mr. Summers says she has a great deal of money of her own. There is no need to sell the house from under her."

The double doors leading to the drawing room were closed, Emily now being considered able to dispense with a chaperon, since Lord Storm was a guest, however unwilling, and she was mistress of Manley Court.

A great gust of wind shook the house as Lord Storm was talking, and one of the doors to the drawing room blew open.

Duke stirred and awoke, and then his beady eyes became fastened on something that lay beyond the doors in the hall.

"I am not afraid of Miss Manley!" said Emily hotly as Lord Storm walked over to close the door.

Duke dived from the sofa and scampered into the hall before Lord Storm could reach the drawing-room door. The dog seized the object of his fixed attention, a large marrow bone, and bounced happily into the drawing room with it, then laid it down on one of the best oriental rugs preparatory to chewing it.

Before his jaws could reach it, Lord Storm had bent down and whipped the bone away from under his nose. Duke gave a low growl and sprang at Lord Storm with his teeth bared. His lordship struck the dog a heavy blow with his arm, and Duke went sailing across the room and landed in a heap in the corner.

"Monster!" shrieked Emily. She flew to Duke and, sitting down on the floor beside him, cradled his head on her lap.

Lord Storm picked up the bone and threw it on the fire, then fastidiously wiped his hands on his handkerchief.

"First the newspaper, now the poor dog's bone!" raged Emily. "Have you gone quite mad? What else are you going to burn? The furniture?"

Seeing that Duke was unharmed, Emily bounced to her feet, trembling with anger, unaware that the anger had been seething and burning in her since the reading of the will and that now it had found a handy target.

"What else?" she went on, striding up to him and stamping her foot. She looked around wildly until her eye fell on the work basket. "Take this, my lord. 'Twould make a *splendid* blaze!" And picking it up, she threw it into the flames.

"Of all the hysterical, foolish . . ." began Lord Storm coldly.

"Oh, hysterical and foolish, *pooh!* You great starched

beast! Take away your fine clothes and what is there to distinguish you from the lowliest peasant?''

She drummed her fists against his chest, quite beside herself.

He seized her wrists and clipped her arms behind her back so that she was pressed against his chest, then looked down into her flushed face, his eyes alight with sudden mockery.

''Would you like to take away my fine clothes and see what I look like, Miss Winters?'' he asked, his voice light and teasing.

''No, I would *not!*'' raved Emily. ''You are nothing but tailoring and pomade and starch. Why, you probably wear corsets.''

He grinned down at her, holding her wrists behind her back prisoner with his one hand and moving his other between their bodies to unfasten his jacket.

''No, I do not wear corsets, Miss Winters. There is nothing between us now but my thin shirt and your thin gown. I can hear your heart beating.''

''Let me go,'' pleaded Emily, shaken by a sudden wave of treacherous passion. *''Let me go!''*

''I think you should pay a forfeit for such behavior,'' he said. ''Kiss me, Miss Winters.''

''I had rather kiss a . . . a . . . a crocodile,'' said Emily wildly.

''No, you would not, for crocodiles have exceedingly sharp teeth and would bite your pretty mouth so.'' He bent his head and took her full bottom lip between his teeth.

''No,'' mumbled Emily against his mouth.

''Yes,'' he said huskily, his lips closing over her own. His hands released her wrists and came up to hold her chin as his mouth moved caressingly over her own.

Then, abruptly, he let her go, standing back, his eyes wary.

"My apologies, Miss Winters," he said stiffly. "My manners are abominable, but the provocation was great."

Emily translated that in her mind into "I'm sorry, Miss Winters. I forgot you were a person of the lower orders."

She felt bereft, shaken and rejected. "Why did you strike Duke and take his bone away?" she asked. She could not meet his eyes but looked at the floor.

"Because, my dear Miss Winters," he said, walking away toward the window and affording her a good view of his elegantly tailored back, "sooner or later someone is going to realize Sir Peregrine's worst fears and murder that brute. I thought it very opportune that a marrow bone should be lying conveniently in the hall.

"The servants would put it in the dog's dish, and no one else in this house would dream of giving that animal a treat. I do not like to speak ill of Sir Peregrine, because he was your father, but that will was downright malicious."

"Indeed! Perhaps you feel Manley Court was left in the wrong hands?"

"It is more a case of a fortune in diamonds being left in the wrong paws," he said, turning around.

There was a low snore, and Emily glared at Duke, who was once more spread out on the sofa fast asleep. He had not budged an inch when Lord Storm was kissing her. His lordship could have been strangling me for all that wretched animal cared, thought Emily bitterly.

"Not a very good guard dog, is he?" asked Lord Storm, reading her thoughts.

"No," agreed Emily. "I would have expected him to have guarded me from unwanted attentions."

Obscurely, she wanted to goad him into some further demonstration, but he looked at her enigmatically and said, "I think it would be better for both of us if you could manage to overlook my lapse in behavior."

Emily gave a chilly nod. There was nothing else to do.

She swung away from him and stared down into the fire, where the charred remains of her work basket were being licked by the yellow flames.

"It is all very well, being rich," she muttered. "But I am not used to being idle. I cannot go out because of the weather. This is going to be a very long day."

"On the contrary, you have plenty to do," he said. "Mr. Summers is in the library, I believe. It would be a good opportunity to sit down with him and discuss the extent of your inheritance and what you mean to do about your future."

"My future?" said Emily blankly. "What future?"

"You are a woman," he said testily. "You will wish to be married and have children, no doubt. A steward, even a good one like Hardy, is all very well, but this estate needs a man to run it."

"Hardy is a man."

"Now you are being deliberately obtuse. It needs an owner. Someone who will keep the land in good heart so that his son will be ready to step into a good inheritance."

"I have not the slightest interest in getting married. And who would marry me? I am illegitimate."

"You will find that illegitimacy, backed by a great house, and estates and the generous yearly income therefrom, is not the disadvantage it would be had you no fortune."

"I would not wish to marry anyone who just wanted to get their hands on Manley Court," said Emily hotly.

"Oh, my dear, dear girl," he drawled. "Be sensible. Who ever heard of anyone marrying for love? You have too much responsibility now. You need someone with a fortune to match your own so that your estates will continue to prosper. You need—"

"I think I need to sell the whole lot, lock, stock and barrel—and perhaps *enjoy* myself a little."

He remained silent. Duke snored, the fire crackled, and the clocks ticked.

"You talk of marriage," went on Emily. "But the circumstances of my birth certainly prevent anyone like yourself from marrying me."

"Perhaps," he said in a considering voice, talking more to himself than to her. "I have a responsibility to my name, to my—"

"To your arrogance, to your false pride," Emily finished for him. "Oh, yes. You would gladly offer me your protection were I not mistress of this house. But you would never marry me."

"One would almost think you were trying to goad me into a proposal," he said.

"I would not have *you*," sneered Emily, wild with hurt. "You with your groping hands and . . . and . . ."

"And my corset. Let us not forget my corset."

"Rot your corset, sir!" said Emily, working herself into a passion again.

"Dear me! What are you shouting about, Miss Winters? You're nose is turning quite red with emotion," said a light, amused voice as the vision that was Clarissa Singleton floated into the room.

She wrinkled up her pretty nose. "Ugh! What a foul odor, and the fire is full of black stuff. What have you been burning? Dead dog, by any chance? Or is that too much to hope for?"

Lord Storm's eyes were alight with mocking humor as he made his bow to Clarissa. "Dear madam," he said, kissing her hand. "Miss Winters and I were having a little Guy Fawkes party. Duke, as you can see, is sound in wind and limb. Does he plan to wear all those diamonds, Miss Winters?"

"No," mumbled Emily, feeling like a sulky child.

Clarissa's beauty and poise made Emily feel very young and gauche.

Duke slid down from the sofa and ambled, yawning, over to Emily and shoved his wet nose in her hand. "I must take him out," said Emily.

"My dear Storm, let me tell you the latest *on-dit*," cooed Clarissa, leading him to the sofa vacated by Duke.

She sat down and patted the place next to her invitingly. He sat down and leaned toward her. Clarissa seemed to take his whole interest.

"I'm going, my lord," said Emily from the doorway.

Clarissa bent her flaming head close to Lord Storm's and began to talk in a low voice.

"*I'm going,*" said Emily again, but neither looked up, and so she trailed off miserably with Duke at her heels.

After she had exercised Duke in the comparative shelter of the kitchen garden, she began to think that it might not be such a bad idea to discuss her future with Mr. Summers.

When Duke had been rubbed down and fed, Emily made her way to the library with the dog at her skirts.

Mr. Summers surveyed her over his pince-nez and rose hurriedly to his feet. "My dear Miss Winters! I was wondering whether we should have a chance to talk, but I felt perhaps you should be allowed to get over the shock you have received. Poor lady! I wish I had been able to break the news of your birth to you in a more conventional manner, but your father was an unfeeling man in many ways. Oh, well, *De mortuis nil nisi bonum*.

"It was a distressing thing to do, leaving that fortune to the dog. Most of the diamonds are single gems, you know. They have not been set into any jewelry as yet. They are locked up in the bank in London, and I suggest you should leave them there for safekeeping. As I told Mr. and Mrs. Manley, a dog does not have a very long life at the best of times, but they did not seem to be consoled. Now, how can I help you?''

Emily sat down in a chair by the fire and leaned her head against the back. She looked very young and very tired. Duke stretched out at her feet. Emily looked around the room, at the firelight flickering over the gold lettering and calf binding of the books which lined the walls, and remembered another library and a happier day.

''I don't know,'' she said dully. ''I must put my life in some sort of order, but I cannot stay here. I wish to sell Manley Court, but Lord Storm says I must consider the welfare of the tenants and servants. But surely they would be just as happy with another landlord?''

''Not necessarily, particularly these days,'' said Mr. Summers.

He placed the tips of his fingers together and surveyed her over the steeple made by them.

''There are a great many absentee landlords among the aristocracy. They live in London and hardly ever visit their estates in the country.

''I personally feel that if a man—or a woman—draws a large income from an estate, then he or she has a responsibility toward every soul on that estate. But you are very young, and this responsibility has fallen on your shoulders very suddenly. I have a suggestion to make. Why don't you go away for a little?''

''Where?'' said Emily blankly. ''I have no friends, apart from a few poor souls left back at the orphanage, and I have no relatives. I refuse to think of any of the Manleys as my relatives.''

The lawyer scratched his wig in perplexity, and then his face cleared.

''I have a sister living in Bath,'' he said. ''She is Lady Bailey. She is a widow. Her husband, Sir Desmond Bailey, was an army man. She lives very quietly but would enjoy some young company, and she would sponsor you at the assemblies in Bath.

"Your first duty, of course, Miss Winters, should be to consider marriage to some suitable man who will take the reins from your hands. The fair sex," he said with a comic little bow in her direction, "were not put on this earth to run businesses or estates or anything of that nature. It is the duty of every woman to be the guiding light of some gentleman and fill his nursery with children."

"Oh, I suppose so," said Emily fretfully. It was certainly unheard of in her small and inexperienced world that a woman should do anything of an administrative nature. "But my duty, my duty. Have I no duty to myself?"

"Duty can be pleasurable," said Mr. Summers. "Balls and assemblies and routs are the . . . hem . . . natural overture to marriage. Come, Miss Winters, you are an attractive young lady! Surely you wish to go to balls and parties?"

"I suppose so," said Emily. "But what of my birth? Surely the high sticklers in Bath will look down their long noses at me!"

"There is no reason why anyone should know that you were not born in wedlock. Miss Manley and Mr. James Manley do not wish such a fact about their brother to come to light. Mrs. Singleton can be advised to keep silent, and the Misses Kiplings. I have no doubt the Kiplings will shortly find an excuse to come on a visit once they have received my letter with the terms of the will."

"And no doubt they will all try to kill Duke."

"I have no doubt," said Mr. Summers. "I should certainly try to kill the animal myself if he stood between me and a fortune in diamonds. He is only a dog, and a very ill-favored one at that."

"Duke is like me—a mongrel," said Emily, experiencing the first twinges of loyalty to the dog. "I think I shall consider your kind offer, Mr. Summers. It might be as well to remove myself—and Duke—as far from Manley Court as possible. But," she added, "give me until tomorrow to make up my mind. Now, I shall need to know how to go about getting funds to buy clothes and such things."

"Certainly, Miss Winters. If you will join me at this table, I will explain to you how you go about obtaining funds. . . ."

After a grueling two hours, Emily left the library with her head spinning. Apart from a fortune in ready money, she not only owned Manley Court but a town house in St. James's and a shooting box in Yorkshire and property in the City of London itself.

She went quietly upstairs to her room. A gust of wind slashed rain against the window. Thaw. If it continued to rain like this all night, then Lord Storm would be gone in the morning.

Her body ached in a most peculiar way at the memory of his kisses. But he *had* kissed her and held her, despite the fact that he did not want to. Slowly Emily began to experience a heady feeling of power.

She sat down in front of the looking glass, noticing the sheen of her heavy black hair and the wide depths of her blue eyes for the first time.

Why go to Bath? she mused. It would be much more fun to stay here and tame Lord Storm. With any luck, Clarissa and Harriet would keep to their rooms and she would be able to dine alone with him.

But both Clarissa and Harriet were present in the drawing room with Lord Storm when Emily entered. Harriet went on as if Emily did not exist, and Clarissa talked exclusively to Lord Storm, her large eyes caressing him. And Lord Storm?

He looked at Clarissa as if she were the only woman in the world. Ignoring Emily's prior claim, he led Clarissa to dinner. They laughed and chatted about plays Emily had never seen, music she had never heard, and people she had never met.

Clarissa had dropped her former show of friendliness to Emily. It was obvious she was feeling very sure of her powers of attraction.

Emily sat silent and miserable. Lord Storm had not meant anything by his caresses. He looked at that moment as if the only woman he wanted to kiss was Clarissa Singleton.

For one brief second he raised his eyes and looked at Emily from under hooded lids. She flushed like a school-girl and looked at her plate.

How Emily longed to smile and be witty and sparkle. But what could she talk about? The weather? The girls at the orphanage?

At last the weary meal dragged to its close, and the ladies retired to leave his lordship to enjoy his wine in solitary splendor.

Lord Storm sat twisting his glass around and around in his fingers. He knew he had behaved very badly, but Miss Emily Winters was in need of a set-down. He had to admit to himself that she had made his pulses race in a most uncomfortable way. But she was little more than a school-girl and quite unsuitable. With any luck, the roads would be clear, and, when he saw her again, *if* he saw her again, it would be at some county affair where he would be obliged only to be distantly polite to her. For a moment he remembered the happy, smiling girl he had taken driving and how the frozen waterfall had burned in the sun.

He resolutely put the picture from his mind. He had been momentarily seduced because of the proximity forced on them by the storm.

But when he finally entered the drawing room and she was not there, he felt a stab of disappointment and behaved very formally and correctly to Clarissa, who endured his chilly manners for quite half an hour before asking him when they could expect a visit from his friend Mr. Harris.

A violent rainstorm during the night did much to clear the roads, and Lord Storm estimated he could safely reach his home on horseback. He would have his carriage sent over when the weather grew better.

He sent his compliments to Miss Winters by Rogers, requesting to see her for a few moments to say goodbye.

But after what seemed like a very long time, Rogers returned with the intelligence that Miss Winters sent her compliments to his lordship and her best wishes for a speedy and safe journey, but begged to be excused.

Later, John Harris reflected he had never seen his friend in quite such a temper. All Lord Storm would say on his return was that he was well quit of Manley Court and never wanted to see any of them again.

John wisely let matters rest, deciding to ride over to Manley Court at the first opportunity to find out how matters stood for himself.

Chapter Five

"*I am not suggesting we plunge into a life of eternal* dissipation, my dear Miss Winters," said Lady Bailey, "I am only suggesting something a tiny bit more lively than taking that reprehensible mongrel for walks. He bit my poor footman, John, in the calf the other day, which caused a terrible commotion—not to mention the price of a new pair of silk stockings."

"I'm sorry, Lady Bailey," said Emily wanly. "I am not much company for you, I'm afraid."

"Oh, *any* company is better than my own," said her ladyship. "But *do* consider how dull it is for me, my dear, and make some push to be gay."

Lady Bailey was about seventy, but very small, very quick, and very spry. Emily had been resident with her for nearly three months. At first, Lady Bailey had been delighted to go about with Emily to all the dressmakers and milliners and mantua makers, but after Emily had amassed a quite considerable wardrobe of pretty clothes, she had seemed determined not to show them off at any social occasion.

In despair, Lady Bailey had invited the grandchildren of her old friends, who were all about Emily's age, to a musical evening. But Emily had pleaded the headache and had gone to her room.

Spring had, it seemed, flown over the hills during the night and had arrived in Bath at last, a warm frivolous wind tugging fleecy clouds across the sky and sending skirts and parasols twirling.

Bath was no longer in its heyday, but the predominant desire was still to "cut a dash." Everything seemed to have turned into bustle and gaiety with the advent of the warm weather, and spring had also flown into Lady Bailey's old bones and made her long for crowds and gossip.

Lady Bailey had questioned Emily closely about Manley Court and its occupants and had at last elicited the information that Lord Storm had been a guest. By Emily's blush and by the way the girl seemed anxious not to mention his lordship's name, Lady Bailey thought she had at last discovered Emily's problem.

And so, on this bright sunny morning, with the daffodils dancing in the square outside and the windows open to let in the sweet air, Lady Bailey moved directly to the attack.

"I want to talk about Bartholomew Storm," she said abruptly, her sharp black eyes in her wrinkled face noticing the telltale blush spreading up Emily's cheeks.

"You mentioned he was a house guest at Manley Court. It is a good thing you are such a sensible girl or I would think you had fallen madly in love with him like so many other silly little girls."

"Many?" queried Emily faintly.

"Oh, dear me, yes. A terrible rake was Storm before he went to the wars, and I doubt his experiences have changed him any. A terrible rake, my dear, and quite ruthless with women. Not, mind you, that he ever bothered himself with any of our debutantes. But quite a tragedy happened. His mother, Honoria, came to take the waters once, just before he joined the army, and Storm came to Bath with her.

"He danced very prettily at the assemblies and promptly set up a liaison with a certain lady whose bloodline was as excellent as her morals were bad. But there was this charming young debutante, Cecily Manning, who fell madly in love with him. Not that he did anything to encourage her that anyone could see, but he did not exactly do anything to *discourage* her either. And so this Cecily built it up in her mind that he was really madly enamored of her but could not do anything about it because he was in the clutches of his mistress. So the silly thing sneaked herself into his house one night and hid on his bedchamber. Well, fortunately for her, he did not come home that night, but she was discovered by the servants and her parents were sent for and there was a terrible to-do and scandal."

"And what happened to Cecily?"

"Well, the Mannings were Roman Catholic, so they simply tucked her away in a convent, which all goes to show how very useful the Catholic religion can be. But that is the trouble with silly little girls. They have only to clap eyes on a hardened rake and they convince themselves that they are the very ones to reform him. Now isn't that *stoopid?*"

"Very," said Emily in a colorless voice.

"And I really hope he does not show that devilishly handsome face here again, because it's just like a fox getting into the hen coop. Such a fluttering and screeching. I heard Honoria is to come to take the waters, but she does not approve of her son at all, and she blamed him publicly. Will Lord Storm—if he comes—be surprised to find you living like a nun, I wonder?"

Lady Bailey noticed the sudden flash in Emily's eyes

with satisfaction, so she rattled on, "Of course, you must make up your mind to leaving Duke behind. You simply cannot start taking that animal to balls. I know you are afraid for his life. But none of the people who hope to inherit the diamonds is present in Bath. He will do very well with the servants."

Emily's soft mouth folded into a rebellious line. "I could not possibly enjoy myself knowing Duke to be a pray to every danger. I would rather hire a burly guard especially to take care of the animal."

"Oh, very well," said Lady Bailey. "You know, you hate those Manleys so much that you don't even want the hound to die a *natural* death. But the fault lies not all on the Manley side but on your own."

"I?" Emily stared. "I have done nothing."

"No?" queried Lady Bailey with a lift of her false eyebrows. "Only think. Sir Peregrine chooses to bring a girl from an orphanage into his home without so much as a by-your-leave. Then he goes and leaves his entire estate to this girl, who turns out to be his daughter. I feel quite sorry for the Manleys."

"They were very unkind to me *before* Sir Peregrine's death," said Emily in a low voice.

"Of course they were," said Lady Bailey robustly. "You carry around with you that air of meek innocence. Enough to turn anyone cruel. You must not appear so vulnerable. Try to be a little haughty. Tilt your chin so, and look down your nose." Duke, who had come to life during the proceedings, suddenly lifted his head in a grotesque parody of Lady Bailey and looked down his nose.

Emily burst out laughing. "That's better," said Lady Bailey. "If you cannot achieve hauteur, then some animation will do nicely. 'Tis such a monstrous funny thing, but do you know that at one time I actually thought you were pining for Storm? La! How foolish of me. But that was before I knew you for the sensible young lady you are.''

And having pinned Emily with that final shaft, Lady Bailey arose and shook out the skirts of her taffeta gown. ''I shall send John to you and you may ask him if he would like to take on the extra duty of guarding Duke. If he will not, ask him to get you someone.''

When the energetic old lady had bustled off, Emily moved to a chair by the open window and looked out at the sunny square. Green leaves shifted and turned and glinted like enamel in the sun and the wind. The terrible winter was over and the world was young again.

It was not that she was in love with Lord Storm, thought Emily. The pain at her heart was because he had humiliated her first socially and then as a woman.

Lady Bailey was right. She would not hide away. Thoughts came tumbling one after the other through her mind like the great white clouds tumbling across the pale-blue sky above. She, Emily, had made absolutely no move to assert herself before she left Manley Court. Harriet still took the head of the table, ordered the meals, and directed the household. And it's *my* house! she thought with growing rebellion. Harriet was not in the least conciliatory to me, because she thinks I am too spineless to put her out. Well, I shall cut my social teeth in Bath and learn some poise, and *then* let Miss Harriet Manley beware!

The door opened, and John, one of Lady Bailey's footmen, came in. ''You wanted to see me, miss?''

Emily nodded and outlined her plan for the guardianship of Duke. A look of ludicrous dismay crossed the footman's face. Like quite a number of servants, he was more snobbish than his mistress. Pictures of walking that ugly mongrel while James, his rival next door, walked Lord Bellamy's exquisite poodle did not bear thinking of.

"I am not at all good with animals, miss," he said, tugging nervously at his claret-and-silver livery.

"It would be extra wages for you, of course," pointed out Emily.

For one minute, the footman's eyes brightened, but then they fell on the black-and-gold lump of fur that was Duke, and he sighed. "No, miss, I don't want to seem unobliging, but me and dogs never see eye to eye."

"Then you can suggest one of the servants?"

John's face cleared with relief. "Certainly, miss. I will send someone to you directly."

Emily waited and waited. Two young misses and their maids walked along outside, muslin skirts fluttering in the spring wind. A smart phaeton pulled up and two gentlemen raised their hats. The girls curtsied and giggled.

That was youth out there, thought Emily. All set for flirtations and love letters and hopes and fears of marriage. And here she was, still seventeen, and already older in her manner than Lady Bailey.

The door opened and a small boy was pushed in. He could not have been more than twelve. He had a round, red, scrubbed face and hair that stuck up all over his head like a porcupine's quills. He looked as if he had just been subjected to a scrubbing under the pump, which indeed he had.

"This here is Jimmy Jenkins, knife boy and pot scrubber to her ladyship," the footman said. "He's eager to look after the dog, miss." And with that, John gave the knife boy another shove into the center of the room and then made his escape.

Jimmy stood with his hands behind his back, looking at the pattern of twisting dragons on the oriental rug. Emily looked at the lad.

"How old are you Jimmy?" she asked.

"Thirteen, please, miss."

"You look younger."

"I'm small for me age, please, miss."

"Well, Jimmy," said Emily doubtfully, "I shall tell you a story about Duke. Duke is my dog. Sir Peregrine Manley died and left a fortune in diamonds to this dog. If anything should happen to the dog, then a number of greedy Manley relatives will get their hands on that fortune. Now, I cannot be with Duke every minute of the day, and I want someone to guard him at all times. You do not look very strong." She hesitated. "It would be necessary to take you away from your kitchen duties, but . . . oh, I really do think a full-grown man would be better!"

"If you please, miss," said Jimmy dismally. For one brilliant sunny moment, Jimmy's future had seemed to stretch out golden and blissful before him. And now it was snatched away.

Emily felt a pang of pity as she looked at the boy's bent head. In a way he was like Duke, scrubby and ill favored. Perhaps she could make him a page. It seemed such a shame to send him back to the kitchens.

Then Duke arose from his comfortable sleep beside the fire. He stretched and looked around. His close-set eyes became fixed on the boy who stood miserably in the middle of the room. Slowly Duke's tail began to wag. To Emily's amazement, Duke ambled across the room and reared himself up, placed his paws on Jimmy's shoulders, and licked his face.

It was too much for Jimmy. He was genuinely fond of animals and thought the dog was trying to comfort him, and so he put his arms around Duke and buried his scrubbed red face in Duke's rough coat and cried and cried. And Duke, sensing the distress of his new friend, threw back his head and began to howl dismally. The noise was terrible.

"Stop it, both of you!" shouted Emily with her hands to

her ears. "Yes, yes, yes, Jimmy, you may have the job. Duke obviously likes you."

Jimmy raised a tear-stained, glowing face. Duke stopped howling. Both of them stared at Emily. Both had close-set, small eyes with a wary look.

"Now, Jimmy," said Emily severely, "I think you should start your duties right away. Send Dayton, the butler, to me. We must discuss with him the change in position." She looked at his ragged knee breeches, which had once done service for a fully grown man and were now hitched up somewhere around Jimmy's dirty neck cloth. "And I think you should have new clothes."

Jimmy nodded and gulped and detached himself from Duke's embrace.

Duke followed him as far as the door and then slumped down with his nose between his paws as if aware that his new friend would shortly return.

Jimmy's elevation in the ranks caused no jealousy among the servants. Not one of them wanted the job of taking care of Duke, and so in no time at all, Jimmy found himself possessed of two new suits of sober black, four shirts, two new pairs of shoes, and a bed in the footmen's dormitory at the top of the house.

Although Emily had no immediate social engagements, Jimmy was obviously eager to begin his duties, and so she allowed Jimmy to take the dog out. She watched the boy and Duke walking sedately to the end of the square in the tender blue light of an early spring evening. As soon as they reached the end of the square, Jimmy shouted something and began to run down the long cobbled hill that led away from the center of the town, with Duke barking and leaping about him.

Emily stood and watched them until they were out of sight, experiencing a pang of pure envy at their carefree freedom.

*   *   *

Emily found her first ball in Bath's famous Pump Room quite a disappointment, but she would not even admit to herself that it was because she secretly hoped that a certain autocratic lord with white-gold hair and cynical gray eyes would be there.

She was a great success and danced very prettily with a number of eligible gentlemen. Soon carriages were calling at Lady Bailey's narrow house in Somerset Square, and Emily put on such a great show of flirting and laughing with her beaux that even the sharp-eyed Lady Bailey was forced to think she had been mistaken in assuming that Miss Winters was pining for Lord Storm.

As the days grew longer and warmer and the social round increased in pace, Emily began to forget Lord Storm. Her most assiduous gallant was a young gentleman by the name of Guy Wayne-Viking. Mr. Wayne-Viking was refreshingly ordinary, from his pleasant open features to his sandy hair, modest dress, and uninteresting conversation. Soon Emily was standing up with him for at least two dances at the assemblies, and the Bath gossips whispered that Miss Winters and Mr. Wayne-Viking were shortly to make a match of it.

Duke, meanwhile, was glossy and happy and forever absent in the company of Jimmy.

The first cloud appeared on Emily's horizon in the shape of the Misses Kiplings. They had certainly not come to Bath to see Emily; they cut her as dead as they could. Then Honoria, Countess of Freham, and Lord Storm's mother, arrived to take the waters. Emily studied her with interest as she walked in the Pump Room one morning with Lady Bailey. The countess did not look at all like her tall, handsome son. She looked small and dumpy and exceedingly bad-tempered.

Then the cloud of foreboding grew darker one evening

shortly after Fanny and Betty Kipling's arrival. Dayton, Lady Bailey's butler, informed Miss Winters that Jimmy was talking some nonsense about a beautiful lady who had tried to poison Duke.

Jimmy was sent for and arrived with the doting Duke lolling at his heels.

"What is this I hear?" demanded Emily. "I hope my tale of vengeful relatives has not affected your imagination, Jimmy."

"No, miss," said Jimmy. "It was like this here. . . ." And he began to tell his story.

It appeared that he had been teaching Duke tricks in a field on the outskirts of town. Then they had been racing and playing. A very fine carriage had drawn up alongside and a lady had called him over. No, he couldn't quite describe her, because she was wearing a bonnet and a veil. She had asked him if he would like a chocolate and said he could have one for his dog.

Now, if Jimmy had been older, perhaps he might not have taken Emily's warning so seriously. But it all seemed so exciting to him that he, Jimmy, was in sole charge of a dog who owned a fortune, and he had been on the constant lookout for trouble, and so he had firmly refused the chocolates. At that moment, Duke had come bounding up to the carriage.

The lady had laughed and said she was sure the dog would love chocolate, and she threw one to Duke, shouting, "Catch!" "Well, miss," said Jimmy, "Duke caught it in his mouth but I fell on 'im and shoved his jaws apart and drug it out, like. The lady slams the carriage door shut and shouts to her driver to move along. I takes out me penknife and cuts the chocolate in half and there's this nasty gooey stuff i' the middle."

"Chocolates are like that, Jimmy," said Emily, guessing that the boy had never had a chocolate in his life. "But you were very wise to be cautious."

"But it do smell funny. See, miss, I got it here." He dug into a capacious pocket and came out with a twist of paper, which he carefully unwrapped. Emily sniffed the chocolate. It had a strange bitter smell. A hand of fear seemed to clutch her stomach, and she stared at Jimmy wide-eyed.

"See, miss, it do be strange, that smell," said Jimmy importantly. "Reckon it was one of these here relatives out for to murder poor Duke."

"It's possible, Jimmy," said Emily faintly. "You may go now. Leave Duke here with me. He may stay with me until I leave for the assembly this evening."

But Duke set up a howl when it looked as if he would be parted from his beloved Jimmy. "Oh, go along with you then, you ungrateful dog," said Emily, half amused, half irritated at the dog's rejection of her.

Jimmy hesitated. "He can do marvelous tricks now, miss. He's that clever, is Duke. Please, miss, would you like to see them?"

"Very well," said Emily, glancing at the clock. Mr. Wayne-Viking was calling to escort her to the ball, but she still had a full hour to get ready.

"Right!" said Jimmy importantly. "Beg for your supper, Duke!" Duke obeyed. "Roll over and play dead." Duke rolled over and stretched out on the carpet with his eyes closed.

"Do a dance for the lady, Duke." To Emily's surprise, Duke rose up on his hind legs and began to waltz slowly around and around with a silly grin on his face.

"Why, that is marvelous, Jimmy," said Emily, when she had finished applauding. "However did you make him do such things?"

"He knows I'm fond of him," said Jimmy gruffly. "We're a pair, me an' Duke."

And indeed they did look a pair as boy and dog gazed at each other in mutual admiration out of their close-set eyes.

Emily questioned Jimmy again about the lady with the chocolates, but apart from a vague impression that she had been young and beautiful, Jimmy could not supply any further information.

It could not be Harriet and certainly not James," thought Emily as she was dressed by her maid. But it could well be either Clarissa or Betty or Fanny.

The clatter of carriage wheels on the cobbles outside brought her to the present. Mr. Wayne-Viking had arrived.

Emily knew she was looking her best in a frock of French net over white satin, painted with a design of red roses. Her hair was piled up in glossy curls and embellished with a circlet of red silk roses. Her scarlet dancing shoes were of the finest kid. It all seemed to have cost a horrendous amount of money, but Emily comforted herself with the thought that her extravagance was not about to reach the astronomical heights achieved by the Empress Josephine, who spent, in one year, three thousand francs on rouge alone.

Mr. Wayne-Viking was dressed in his usual correct manner—neat but not gaudy. His evening suit consisted of a double-breasted dark-blue coat with large yellow double gilt buttons, a white marseilles waistcoat, light brown kerseymere breeches tied with strings at the knees, white silk stockings, and shoes with silver buckles. His stock was neatly tied, and the frill on his cambric shirt was of a modest size.

His eyes lit up when he saw Emily, and Lady Bailey smiled her approval. She thought Mr. Wayne-Viking a very good sort of young man and was looking forward to bragging to her brother about how she had secured a good match for Emily.

In the darkness of the carriage, he pressed Emily's hand and whispered, "There is something I must ask you before this evening is out, Miss Winters."

Emily smiled demurely. She knew he was going to ask her to marry him, and she had quite made up her mind to accept him.

He was a friendly, undramatic young man. She felt at home with him. He did not make her pulses race as the reprehensible Lord Storm had done. That was Mr. Wayne-Viking's main attraction for Emily. He made her feel like a lady.

Emily knew that real ladies were not subject to these awful trembling, stomach-lurching fits of lust. She knew, therefore, that in some way Lord Storm brought out the side of her that must be suppressed.

As Emily alighted from the carriage under the imposing entrance to the Pump Room, she could hear the faint sweet strains of the orchestra. And then all at once, she felt Lord Storm's warm lips caressing her own and his hard body pressed tight against hers. It was so real, so vivid, that Emily could hardly believe she had imagined the whole thing. But there was no Lord Storm, only Mr. Guy Wayne-Viking smiling at her dotingly and stretching out a hand to help her down from the carriage.

He is haunting me, thought Emily, and then, with a superstitious shiver, she thought, I hope he is not dead!

"You are quite pale, Miss Winters," said Mr. Wayne-Viking anxiously. He pressed her hand quite fiercely to show his concern. Privately he thought Emily had probably taken a chill. Ladies wore so little these days, and certainly Emily's whole toilette was so fine and gauzy that he was sure he could roll the whole thing up like a handkerchief and put it in his pocket.

As Emily entered the colonnaded ballroom with its great glittering chandeliers, the first person she saw was Clarissa Singleton, who did not seem to be in the slightest aware that red hair was desperately unfashionable—apart from the Scotch, and who took account of them?—or care that no one had ever liked hair that terrible color. The Duke of Wellington's son had red hair, and his grace so loathed the color that he had taken to shaving the boy's eyebrows! But Clarissa's hair burned like a flame, and the gentlemen fluttered about her like so many moths willing to be burned.

Mr. Wayne-Viking led Emily across to where his mother was sitting with the dowagers. Emily did not like Mrs. Wayne-Viking. She was a fat, petulant woman, forever complaining. After exchanging a few pleasantries with her, Mr. Wayne-Viking and Emily took their places for a country dance.

Halfway through the dance, Emily felt a hostile emanation which seemed to be directed toward her from the north side of the room. She glanced across in that direction, and her step faltered. Clarissa was surveying her, her eyes bright with malice. And from Clarissa, two little streams of gossip seemed to run around the perimeter of the room. Head bent toward head, faces registered shock, lorgnettes and quizzing glasses were raised, until it seemed to Emily as if a forest of accusing eyes were staring at her.

And then she knew: Clarissa had talked! The secret of her illegitimacy was broadcast in Bath.

"Guy! Come here this minute!"

The strident tones of Mrs. Wayne-Viking cut across the music.

"What on earth is up with mother?" asked Mr. Wayne-Viking. "I fear she may be suffering an attack. But how can we leave the set? The dance is nearly over. Come with me, Miss Winters."

But Emily thought she knew what the matter was with Mr. Wayne-Viking's mama. She decided to let him find out for himself and invented a tear in her gown that must be urgently repaired.

As she made her way to an anteroom set aside for such feminine disasters, she decided not to flee the ball. Guy was in love with her. He would explain that to his mother. When she returned, he would have had time to talk to his mother, and then he would take her hand and lead her to the supper room, just as if nothing had happened. Mr. Wayne-Viking was a true gentleman, thought Emily, swallowing a lump in her throat.

Bartholomew Storm leaned against a pillar in the corner and waited for Emily to return. He had heard the whispers and was busy wondering what he could do to counteract the scandal caused by the malicious Clarissa.

He had been in Bath a few days and had heard of the impending engagement between Emily and Mr. Wayne-Viking. He glanced across the room to where Mr. Wayne-Viking was in agitated conversation with his mother. He seemed, thought Lord Storm, to be a very sensible sort of fellow—at least sensible enough not to do anything so cruel as to snub her. Meanwhile Lord Storm congratulated himself on his detached feelings for Emily. He had to admit that he had thought of her quite a lot, but he always managed to remind himself that her unfortunate birth made her thoroughly unsuitable. He also had to admit that her beauty had given him quite a jolt when he had first seen her in the ballroom. She had acquired a new poise and grace that were quite enchanting. It was as well he was a hardened bachelor, for he had also decided that since he had a young cousin who would make a suitable heir, there was no need to spoil his bachelor life by getting married just for the sake of a son.

And then Emily returned.

There was a slight flush on her face and her large eyes were glinting with unshed tears, but she held her head high and walked toward Mr. Wayne-Viking. How quiet the room seemed. How every eye seemed to be avidly fixed on her.

The dancers were promenading the room, waiting for the first chords of the waltz.

Emily said something to Mr. Wayne-Viking, a little smile pinned bravely on her mouth.

Mr. Wayne-Viking turned his back on her. It was the cut direct.

Emily's face flamed. She turned on her heel, her eyes wild. Lord Storm knew she was about to run from the ballroom.

He walked smartly across the ballroom floor and clipped an arm around her waist as the first chord struck.

"My waltz, I think, Miss Winters," he said firmly. "No!" he added in a savage undertone. "You will not run away. You will laugh and flirt with me and we shall confound Clarissa before this evening is out."

Emily stumbled against him. He swept her into the steps of the waltz. "Dance, Miss Winters," he urged. "Only see how jealous and furious Mrs. Singleton is!"

And Emily danced, held rather more tightly than the conventions allowed. The room swirled around her, and suddenly she knew that as long as he did not let go of her, she could bear anything.

"You are the most beautiful woman in the room, Miss Winters," he said. "Smile at me!"

But Emily stared at his top waistcoat button, frightened to lift her eyes in case she saw cruelty and mockery in his.

"If you do not smile, Miss Winters, I shall kiss you in the middle of the Pump Room, and then you really will be ruined."

At that she raised her eyes. His own gray ones were looking down at her intently. "Pretend I am Duke and look as if you love me," he said. "How is that dreadful mongrel, by the way? Has anyone killed him yet?"

"No," whispered Emily. "I—I think someone tried. At least Jimmy said they did."

"Jimmy? Who is Jimmy?"

Emily fell silent again, still smarting and hurting.

"I said, who is Jimmy?" he demanded. "Talk! Laugh! Smile! Don't tell me you have no backbone."

Instead Emily said in a low voice, "I think he was going to propose marriage to me—Mr. Wayne-Viking, that is. I never thought he . . . he . . ."

"You are about to cry. Don't. I do not want you to soil your pretty lips with the name of that popinjay. Tell me about the attempted murder of Duke or I shall shake it out of you. You have only me to worry about. After this dance we shall have supper. And after supper, I shall take you home. So talk!"

Haltingly at first, but finally gaining courage, Emily began to tell him about Duke. Lord Storm kept laughing appreciatively as if she were telling him some of the wittiest *on dits* he had ever heard, and when he was not laughing he kept staring over her shoulder at Clarissa in a mocking way that made that lady blush angrily.

When the waltz finished, he neatly swung Emily to a stop next to Clarissa.

"Ah, Mrs. Singleton," said Lord Storm, staring insolently down the front of Clarissa's décolletage. "Behind with the gossip as usual. Well, that's one of the penalties one must pay for marrying a Cit. Always trotting out last year's *on dits*."

Clarissa's court gathered around her. Fanny and Betty Kipling crept to the edge of the circle of listeners.

Lord Storm's voice became louder and more insolent.

"Now, take that fascinating bit of rubbish you've been spreading around about Miss Winters being Sir Peregrine Manley's by-blow. Sadly out-of-date. Summers found another will in the library, you know."

Clarissa's eyes gleamed. "You mean all that rubbish about the dog's getting the diamonds is false?"

"Oh, no," said Lord Storm, his voice now carrying around the room. "He left the diamonds to the dog and his considerable fortune to Miss Winters. But he lied about Miss Winters's birth so as to tease you all. What a malicious old gentleman he was, to be sure. No, the old boy actually married a certain royal personage, and so the marriage had to be kept secret. The lady died soon after giving birth. But it was a legal and binding marriage for all that. But I am deeply indebted to you, ma'am, for your antique gossip. It has driven away all the other suitors and left me in sole possession of one of the richest heiresses Bath has ever seen!"

"How was I to know that?" raged Clarissa, her face as red as her hair.

"Perhaps because you did not want to know it. Infuriating, isn't it? Miss Winters is so very beautiful. It seems too much that she should be of royal blood and have all that money as well. Come, my dear Miss Winters. I declare all this gossip has made me devilishly hungry."

The crowd parted to let them through, the ladies dropping Emily very deep curtsies as befitted her royal birth.

At the door of the supper room, a very red-faced Mr. Wayne-Viking was waiting.

"I could not help but hear what his lordship said, Miss Winters," he began. "I most sincerely—"

"Who is this fellow?" demanded Lord Storm, staring at the blushing Mr. Wayne-Viking.

"I haven't the faintest idea," said Emily, and Lord Storm led her past the gaping young man into the supper room.

"Oh, thank you," whispered Emily tremulously.

"Not now," he said in a low voice. "Just remember that being illegitimate has its advantages. It's rather like being poor. It helps you to tell your friends from your enemies."

Emily's heart sank. For one glorious moment she had thought he had been telling the truth about her birth. He had sounded so convincing.

But he teased her and told jokes and made her eat a little, until, to her great relief, he said he would take her home. "I have an open carriage and I will leave you on your doorstep, so there is no need for Lady Bailey to worry about us. It is a good thing my mama is not present. She is the only woman who can see through my lies. I shall scrawl a note to Lady Bailey, and that will save us from the perils of the ballroom. Oh, here she is!"

Emily started to perform the introductions, but Lady Bailey interrupted her. "I know Storm of old. I am grateful to you, my lord, for your work this evening." She turned to Emily.

"Do not think too harshly of young Wayne-Viking. Any man would have behaved the same way faced with such a piece of scandalous gossip."

"Lord Storm did not," said Emily in a low voice.

"Oh, well, Storm's different. He never cared a fig for what the world thought."

"Before you blacken my character further, ma'am," said Lord Storm, "I am escorting Emily home in an open carriage, and I shall only go with her as far as the street door, so you need not trouble—"

"Oh, run along," said Lady Bailey ungraciously. "I

think I have had just about all I can bear. I was so looking forward to telling my brother that Miss Winters was suitably engaged.''

"Come, Miss Winters," said Lord Storm. "It is a pleasant night for a drive. Do you have a cloak?"

"Just my shawl. It will take me a minute to fetch it."

Lord Storm waited at the entrance to the Pump Room for Emily. The Misses Kipling came scampering up. "Dear Lord Storm," cooed Fanny. "Was it not monstrous of Sir Peregrine to leave his diamonds to a dog?"

"Monstrous," he agreed. "But dogs do not live forever, and no doubt the jackals will have them soon enough."

"Oooh, awful man," muttered Fanny. "Come along, Betty. The gentlemen are waiting."

Lord Storm smiled at their retreating backs.

Emily felt it was all strangely familiar to be perched up beside him as he drew on his gloves and took the reins. The cool breeze of the earlier evening had died, leaving the air warm and still and scented with lime and lilac.

She glanced sideways under her lashes at his strong profile and firm chin. Oh, if only he were not such a rake and cared for her a little! Not that she was in love with him. But she wished he were not quite so indifferent to her.

As if conscious of her gaze, he turned his head and looked at her, and she quickly looked away. The wind from the movement of the carriage was whipping her underdress against her legs, outlining their long shape. He felt his pulses beginning to race. There was a full moon shining above, and the whole peaceful night seemed spread out before them. Down a cobbled side street, a linkboy trotted in the distance like a wayward star.

They seemed to be the only people out and about, the clip-clop of the pair of matched bays sending back echoes from the silent houses on either side of the street. They swung down away from Somerset Square.

"Where are we going?" asked Emily in a hushed voice. The night was so quiet that it made any normal level of speech sound like a shout.

"Just to look at the countryside under the moon, Miss Winters. The fresh air will make you sleepy, and you need a good night's sleep after your ordeal."

She felt she should protest, but there was a strange feeling of being safe with him, isolated with him, moving through an empty moonlit dream world.

In a short time, the town was left behind and they took the Corsham road. From the quarries of Corsham had come the marvelous stone that had made Bath a golden city. The huge moon rode high above the crescent of hills surrounding Bath and turned the chalky road into a winding white ribbon.

There was a sound of rushing water. "A waterfall," he said quietly. "But not frozen this time." Storm gently reined in his horses.

So he remembered too, thought Emily.

How quiet it was with only the sound of the rushing water. The moon slid behind a cloud. The darkness seemed secret, warm, intimate.

The horses tossed their silky manes and shuffled, and then were still.

Slowly the cloud edged away from the moon, and his eyes were silver as he looked down at her, and his fingers gleamed white as he reached out his hand and turned her face up to his.

Emily let out a little sigh of submission, her breath as warm and sweet as the night air. He muttered something and released her chin.

"Shall we walk for a little, Miss Winters?" he said lightly. "And then I shall take you home."

Emily nodded bleakly, fighting against a wave of disappointment, a realization that this man had known so many women, had had so much experience. What was so earthshaking and devastating to her was play to him.

He jumped down and came around to her side of the carriage and held up his arms to help her down.

Well, he had meant to behave. But as she bent forward in the moonlight, he saw the deep valley between two perfect breasts, and then she fell down into his arms and he clasped her tightly.

His arms seemed full of woman, breasts pressed against his chest, long slim legs against his legs, hair tumbling down, dark midnight hair, hair clean and scented with lavender water, eyes gazing up into his, mouth bewildered and soft and pleading. . . .

He trapped her mouth under his, and the night went whirling away. He seemed to be losing himself in her. Their bodies were fused together, melting together, dying of passion. He could feel her hardening nipples through the fine stuff of her gown.

He had to have her, had to . . . had to . . . had to . . .

"Dear God!" he muttered savagely, as he dragged his mouth away. "Let me take you home instantly. Miss Winters, I beg of you, you must not entice gentlemen so. We are only human, after all."

He tried to laugh, but his voice was ragged.

Emily stood rigid, her arms hanging at her side. Of course, that was all it was. She was a woman and all too willing. She was offering herself to him on a plate.

"Yes, please take me home," she said in a thin voice.

The drive home was fast and urgent and bumpy and noisy. Gone was the magic of the night. Emily knew she had discovered something awful about herself, and her mind kept thrusting whatever it was away.

He set her down at Somerset Square, lifting her down impersonally this time and holding her well away from him.

Emily muttered goodnight and scurried into the house. All she wanted to do was to escape to the privacy of her room and hide under the bedclothes.

A small figure detached itself from a settle in the hall at her entrance.

"Why, Jimmy!" exclaimed Emily. "What are you doing up so late?"

"Me and Duke thought we would see you was home all right," muttered the boy, touching his forelock.

"Thank you, Jimmy, but you must go to bed now." Emily made a sudden decision. "I must take Duke to Manley Court tomorrow, Jimmy. I am leaving Bath."

"Leaving Bath?" gasped the boy. Emily was too weary to note the effect of her words. Jimmy's face had turned very white.

"Yes, as early in the morning as I can manage. Goodnight, Jimmy." With that, Emily bolted up the stairs.

She tried to fight down the realization that was dawning on her, but it would not be kept at bay. It broke over her head as soon as she had closed the door of her room behind her.

"I love him," she said on a sob. "I must get away from him. He will surely break my heart if I stay here."

Perhaps it might have comforted her a little had she known that Lord Storm stayed out in the street in front of the house for quite a long time after she had left, staring at the shining paintwork of Lady Bailey's front door.

Downstairs in the hall, Jimmy hugged Duke fiercely. It never dawned on him that Emily expected him to accompany her to Manley Court. He thought Duke, the only thing he had ever loved and who loved him back equally, was going to be taken away from him. Duke scampered away from Jimmy a little and then, as if to try to cheer the boy up, stood on his hind legs and waltzed slowly around while great hot tears fell down Jimmy's face.

"I trained you good, Duke boy," sobbed Jimmy. "You're good enough for a circus, that you are. You're good enough for Astley's, darn me if you hain't."

And then he slowly wiped the tears away and scrubbed his nose with his cuff. Somewhere inside his brain a little seed of hope began to take root.

Chapter Six

"Gone!" said Emily in a dazed way. "What o'clock is it?"

" 'Tis eleven o'clock o' the morning," wailed the housemaid who had burst into Emily's room. "We just discovered that Jimmy and the dog is nowheres. Jimmy's bed wasn't slept in, neither. We didn't want to worry you, miss, but we only found out after we all started comparing notes, so to speak, and Lord Bellamy's coachman, what was bringing his lordship home at four o'clock, says he saw the boy carrying a bundle a-walking down the street with the dog at his heels."

"Get my clothes! Get my maid!" cried Emily. "Those wretched Manleys have paid Jimmy. Where is Lady Bailey?"

"Gone in person to report the matter to the magistrate."

Emily hurtled downstairs a bare ten minutes later and nearly collided with Lord Storm, who had just been admitted by Dayton.

Emily forgot she loved him and wanted to escape from him. Ignoring Dayton's scandalized face, she seized his lordship by the hand, dragged him into the drawing room, and slammed the door.

"You've got to help me," she said, clutching hold of his lapels. "Jimmy's run off with Duke. One of those terrible Manleys must have paid him to murder the dog. I know they did!"

"Gently," he said. "You are ruining a perfectly good coat. Now calm down. Come over here and sit down on this sofa next to me, take a deep breath, count to ten, and begin."

But all he could get from Emily was the same thing over and over again. Jimmy had taken Duke. Jimmy had been paid by the Manley's to murder Duke.

He took her hands in his and said gently, "We must take a little time and think before we rush around accusing anyone. There would be no point in the Manleys' paying Jimmy to take the dog away. Duke has to be seen to be dead before they inherit anything. Also, it would be very risky to rely on the discretion of a mere boy. Now, when was the last time you saw Jimmy?"

Emily stared at him wide-eyed. "Last night," she said slowly. "It was last night just after you left me. He was sitting in the hall waiting for me."

"And what did he say?"

Emily frowned. "Nothing much. It was quite touching, really. He said something about waiting up to see that I was safely home."

"And then?" prompted Lord Storm. "What did you say?"

"Nothing much. I told him to go to bed."

"And that was all?"

Emily suddenly blushed and withdrew her hands from

his. "I said I was leaving in the morning for Manley Court and . . . and taking Duke with me."

"And did you say anything about taking Jimmy too?"

"No. I assumed he would know that naturally he would be coming too."

"And does the boy care for the dog?"

"Oh, *very* much. It is marvelous to see them together."

"Then there is your answer," he said, standing up. "Jimmy thought he would lose his position—mark you, it is a great rise in social status for a knife boy. He also thought he was losing the dog."

"Perhaps he has relatives," said Emily eagerly. She rang the bell and waited impatiently until Dayton entered the room. "Dayton! Has Jimmy a mother or father or relatives in Bath that he might go to?"

"No, miss," said the butler. "Jimmy was hired from the workhouse. He's a foundling."

"Thank you, Dayton," said Lord Storm. "That will be all."

When the butler had left the room, he turned to Emily. "I think I should search for Jimmy. I have my carriage, and—"

"Please take me with you," begged Emily. "I can show you some of the places where he played with Duke. And . . . and . . . I could not rest. I should go mad with worry, waiting here. A foundling! Poor boy. Poor Jimmy, poor Duke. We are all unwanted in our way."

It was on the tip of Lord Storm's tongue to say impulsively, "You are wanted by me." But his immense pride kept him quiet, for one could say such a thing only to a girl one intended to marry.

Instead he said, "Make ready quickly, then. I have my racing curricle outside. Hurry! I will wait for you."

Emily fairly ran from the room and reappeared only a short time later attired in a lavender wool carriage dress, very simple, very fitting, and very straight, buttoned from neck to hem with tiny raised buttons. She had a Lavinia hat tied firmly over her black curls.

Once outside, Lord Storm helped Emily into his curricle after dismissing his groom so that the man could search the streets for Jimmy on foot.

The day was stifling and hot, and despite her anxiety and distress, Emily could not help wishing she had put on a lighter dress. The leaves of the trees hung motionless in the heavy air, and clouds of dust rose up behind them as they moved slowly along, searching to right and left, stopping occasionally to ask some wayfarer if he had seen a boy with a dog.

Two promising leads sent them racing off through the countryside, lurching down a network of intricate lanes, only in each case to find neither boy nor dog was the one they wanted.

Lord Storm looked remarkably cool despite the heat. He was wearing a bottle-green single-breasted coat with plated buttons, a gold-and-red-striped waistcoat, and leather breeches with brown top boots. His cravat fell in snowy folds at his throat. His strong hands were steady on the reins.

At last he turned to her and slowed his horses to a trot. "I do not think we are going to find him this way, racing haphazardly around the countryside."

The sky above was becoming increasingly hazy and the air increasingly sticky and humid. Emily had stopped fanning herself, since even that small exertion made her perspire.

"I think we should find a hostelry; maybe some refreshment will help us think of something," he went on, setting his horses to a canter.

They soon reached a small village and stopped at a

wayside inn. The inn parlor proved to be dark and smelly, and so Lord Storm suggested they sit at a rickety table in the weedy inn garden. Emily sipped bitter, watery lemonade and looked at an enormous hedge of thistles bordering the inn garden, wondering why the landlord did not take the scythe to them.

"Now," said Lord Storm, "tell me everything you know about Jimmy."

"Hardly anything." Emily sighed. "I asked Lady Bailey's footman, John, if he would like to earn extra wages guarding Duke, and when he refused, I asked him if one of the other servants would do it. He produced Jimmy, the knife boy. I thought Jimmy too young, but the dog took an immediate liking to the boy. And Jimmy adores Duke, there's no question of that. Why, the tricks he could make that dog do! He even taught Duke how to dance on his hind legs."

Lord Storm put down his glass. "You might have hit on the answer."

"What answer? I mean . . . what . . .?"

"Why! If I were a young boy with no money and no family but had this dog who could dance, the first place I would head for is some sort of fair to sell my services."

Emily looked at him in dawning surprise. "That must be it!" she cried. "Where do we begin to look?"

"Wait here," he said. "I will see if the landlord has a local newspaper."

After some moments, he returned with the paper and spread it out on the table while Emily watched him anxiously.

"There is one at Cryffeham," he said. "That is not far from here, I believe. Now, don't look so excited. It's a long way for a boy to walk. We shall probably find nothing but the usual mummery of fat women and two-headed babies."

As they neared Cryffeham, the horses beginning to tire, exhausted with the heat and the miles of travel, they heard the faint sounds of bustle and music.

The fair was being held in a field outside the small town. It looked gay and pretty from a distance, but as they neared, they could see it was a very ramshackle affair with a few tawdry sideshows and a grass ring in the center cleared for cattle shows, ferret chasing, and various feats of strength.

"I must find a posting house soon and rest the horses," said Lord Storm. "But let us search the fair first."

He threw the reins to a small boy and tossed a coin to him, saying they would not be long. They made their way across the dusty grass toward the sideshows, automatically gravitating to the one that was drawing the biggest crowd.

But it was not a dancing dog being billed but a new droll called "The Cruelty of Atreus"—"the scene wherein Thyestes eats his own children is to be performed by the famous Mr. Psalmanazar, lately arrived from Formosa, the whole supper being set to kettle drums."

"Unless Jimmy has volunteered to be eaten, we shall not find him here," said Lord Storm. "Let us try some of the other booths."

They walked along, reading the boards. There was everything *but* a dancing dog. There was even "a bovine curiosity or double cow," which had "given uncommon satisfaction to the several learned bodies by whom it has hitherto been seen," and "a surprising young mermaid, taken on the shores of Aguapulca."

The sky grew very dark overhead, and from a distance a faint rumble of thunder sounded over the noise and music of the fair. Emily's skin prickled under her wool gown. She was beginning to feel very hungry, having left home without even any breakfast.

Her head began to swim, and she loosened the satin ribbons of her bonnet. "You are feeling faint?" asked Lord Storm anxiously. "Let us leave the search until tomorrow."

"There's a knot of people over there," said Emily. "Let's look."

Putting a strong arm around her waist to support her, Lord Storm led her to where a group of people were standing at the edge of the booths, laughing and clapping.

Lord Storm was tall enough to look over the heads of the crowd. he smiled down at Emily and squeezed her waist. "Jimmy and Duke," he said, laughing. "Safe and well. Wait! Emily!"

But Emily had wrenched herself from his grasp and was pushing her way desperately to the front.

Shaggy gold-and-black fur gleaming, stupid grin on his narrow face, Duke was revolving slowly to the beat of a tambourine held by Jimmy.

The boy saw Emily and dropped his tambourine and threw his arms around the dancing dog. "You ain't going to take Duke away from me," he said fiercely.

"Listen to me, Jimmy," cried Emily, running forward. "I—"

"You leave the lad alone," growled a beefy individual who seemed to belong to the fair. "I took 'im on, and half the takings is mine."

Lord Storm strode into the ring made by the gawking crowd.

"Come along, Jimmy," he said sternly. "You heard your mistress."

"No flash cull is takin' away my bread an' butter," growled the beefy man.

He swung a punch at Lord Storm, who neatly blocked it and retaliated with a punishing left to the man's chin. His assailant rocked on his heels and then charged to the attack like an enraged bull.

Emily had no eyes to admire the way his lordship neatly threw his heavier attacker with a cross-buttock. She had knelt down in the grass beside Jimmy and had put her arms around him.

"Oh, Jimmy," she said. "I wasn't going to leave without you, you silly boy. You can be with Duke always, if you like."

Jimmy stared at her in a dazed way. "Always?" he said. "Me and Duke. Us. Together. An' I'll get *paid* for it?"

"Oh, yes, Jimmy," said Emily, laughing through her tears.

Duke pranced up and licked Emily's face and then Jimmy's face.

"You can beat me if you like, miss," said Jimmy. "I done a bad thing, running away. But I don't care so long as I can have Duke."

"You've caused me a lot of trouble." Emily smiled. "But I shan't punish you."

"Thank you, miss," blubbered Jimmy. "I hain't bin so happy in all me born—"

"Very touching," said Lord Storm's chilly voice.

Emily and Jimmy looked around. The beefy man was stretched out cold on the grass, and his lordship was nursing a pair of bleeding knuckles.

I could have had my brains beaten out, reflected Lord Storm sourly, while that precious threesome lay on the grass hugging each other.

Brushing the grass from her dress, Emily said awkwardly, "I am so grateful to you, my lord. It was a brave thing you did. That man was so large and so powerful, I was frightened to look. I was sure you would be killed. How on earth did you manage to fell a great beast like that?"

"I've had some practice," said his lordship, much mollified, although he had a sneaking suspicion that Emily had forgotten all about him in the joys of reunion and was now trying to placate him. "At least, your former master should wake up to the best takings he's ever had, Jimmy."

The crowd had paid more for the fight than they would have paid to see Duke. The beefy man was beginning to stir, so Lord Storm picked up the hat full of money and placed it on his chest.

There was a sudden brilliant flash and then a tremendous crash of thunder.

"We must find shelter soon," he said, holding on to Emily as the crowd began to stream out of the field. The heavens opened and the rain descended on them with the thunderous roar of a torrent in full spate.

There was another tremendous crack of thunder, and over the heads of the crowd, Lord Storm saw the boy who had been holding his horses taking to his heels. There was another violent crack that shook the air above and the ground below. Lord Storm swore, released Emily, and began to run. But he was too late; horses, carriage, and all had run off.

"Here's a coil," he shouted above the uproar of the storm. "My team has bolted. You there, fellow! Is there a gentleman residing nearby?"

The farmer he had addressed shouted back, "Mr, Booth, Cryffeham Manor," and started to struggle out of the field, which was rapidly turning into a bog under the drumming rain. A wind had sprung up, and the fair people were fighting to take down the sodden, flapping canvas of the booths.

The young mermaid taken on the shores of Aguapulca could be seen struggling out of her fish tail, and the double cow was becoming unglued into two separate miserable beasts.

Lord Storm clutched another man as he ran past. "Cryffeham Manor," he shouted. "Which direction?"

The man shouted something, pointing back down the road from which they had come, tugged his sleeve loose, and ran on.

"Let's go," said Lord Storm. "Give me your hand, Emily. Jimmy, keep close behind us."

Despite the rain and the wreck of her bonnet, Emily felt a little glow inside that he had called her by her first name.

They struggled down the mud of the road, away from the field, blinded by the rain. The trees on either side of the road heaved and groaned in the storm.

Just when they were giving up hope of ever finding the manor, they came to a pair of tall wrought-iron gates. They pushed them open and plunged into the relative shelter of a tree-lined drive. The day had grown as black as night.

"We will need to ask this Mr. Booth for shelter for the night," said Lord Storm. "Let us hope he is not some recluse who dislikes visitors."

The trees began to thin out, giving way to expanses of waterlogged lawn. The house, now visible, turned out to be a small square building of red brick, looking more like a workhouse than a manor.

Lord Storm searched for a bell pull and, finding none, hammered loudly at the door.

There was a long silence, and then at long last they could see the bobbing glimmering light of a candle through the narrow windows on either side of the door.

The door swung open to reveal an elderly gentleman dressed in an old-fashioned chintz coat and knee breeches. His face under the shadow of a great bag wig was lined and gentle, and his eyes had a look of vague innocence.

"Come in! Come in!" he said, standing aside. "I fear it

is a bad time to entertain guests, but you are welcome to
what I have. I am afraid I gave my servants the day and
night off. It is a tradition of the house. Every fair they are
allowed to attend, and then they pass the evening feasting
in the village hall.

"I see you have no maid," went on the old man in his
gentle voice. "I fear I am a stickler for the conventions,
and if I am to offer you shelter . . ."

Lord Storm explained at least part of their plight. He
then took one look at Emily's strained, tired face. "Allow
me to introduce ourselves," he said. "I am Mr. Freham,
this is my wife." Emily stifled a gasp. "Jimmy is our
page, and that bundle of wet fur is our dog, Duke. And
you, I gather, are Mr. Booth?"

"Yes, indeed," said Mr. Booth. "I am glad to entertain
a married couple. I should explain, you see. Last winter,
a lady and gentleman had a carriage accident in the snow
and wished to shelter here for the night. But they were not
married, and so I said the gentleman could stay but the
lady could not. They were not chaperoned, you see. Alas,
we have two hostelries in Cryffeham, but neither has
rooms of any description, being more in the way of common alehouses. I remember the lady and gentleman became quite rude and called me an old Methodist because I
would not countenance their staying together under my
roof.

"This lad may take the dog to the kitchens, where he
will find a fire and towels."

Jimmy nodded. His face had registered no surprise when
Lord Storm had said his name was Freham and that Emily
was his wife. Jimmy was still young enough to consider
that all adults moved in mysterious ways their wonders to
perform. He had Duke, and that was all that mattered.

As Jimmy left for the kitchens with Duke at his heels,

Mr. Booth picked up his candle and said he would show "Mr. and Mrs. Freham" to their bedchamber.

After the first shock of hearing she was supposed to be a married lady, Emily had given up caring. She was too uncomfortable and too tired.

"Normally, I would be able to prepare two bedchambers for you," said Mr. Booth, slowly mounting the stairs in front of them. "But with my servants away carousing, I fear there is only the one chamber made up. But it is only for one night."

He pushed open a door. "Ah, here we are. And the fire has been laid, so you only need to light it. I shall ask that boy of yours to help me with a cold collation. It is all I have."

"You are very kind," said Emily shyly.

"Not at all, Mrs. Freham. I do not get much company. I shall expect you belowstairs in, say half an hour? Good, good." He lit a branch of candles on the toilet table and shuffled out, closing the door behind him.

Lord Storm and Emily were left alone.

He bent to light the fire, and Emily looked around the room. There was a four-poster bed in one corner and a door in the other leading to a dressing room. It was a very masculine room, with a high brass fender around the fire and hunting prints on the walls. A stuffed fox head stared glassily down from over the mantel.

"I wish we had asked the good Mr. Booth whether he had any clothes we could change into," said my lord, looking at Emily's wool dress, which was clinging to her body. "I feel we have troubled him enough, but I do not want to sit down to supper in these wet clothes."

There was a knock at the door, and Mr. Booth entered carrying an armful of clothes. "I hope you will both be able to find something among these. I am afraid they are rather in the way of family cast-offs, but perhaps they will serve.''

Lord Storm took the dressing room to change so as to leave Emily the comfort of the fire.

Emily selected a gown of straw satin of an old-fashioned cut. The undergarments were worn and yellowish but clean, and they smelled faintly of lavender. She dressed quickly and nervously, frightened lest Lord Storm should surprise her before she got her dry clothes on.

But he took a long and tactful time dressing himself, and she was able to dry her hair thoroughly at the fire and then pile it in some semblance of a fashionable coiffeur on top of her head.

Lord Storm made his appearance finally. He looked strangely old-fashioned in a long coat of light-brown velvet figured in red and green, worn with knee breeches and high-heeled shoes with enormous buckles.

Emily was glad to escape with him from the enforced intimacy of the bedroom. As they went downstairs, he whispered to her, ''Try to remember we are man and wife or the prim Mr. Booth will have us all sleeping in a hedgerow.''

She nodded in reply, although her heart hammered uncomfortably at the thought of the night to come. Where would they sleep? They could not possibly sleep together.

Supper was a merry affair, since Lord Storm set himself to please, regaling Emily and Mr. Booth with tales of the strange eccentrics he had met on his visits to country houses.

''I never knew anyone to drink quite so much as Lord Saye of Sele,'' said Lord Storm. ''He is a tremendous epicure, and I remember one of his breakfasts where we all dined on omelette made entirely from golden pheasants' eggs. But he would drink absinthe and curaçao in quite terrible quantities. Once when we were going out to dinner, he told his servant, 'Place two bottles of sherry by my bedside and call me the day after tomorrow.'

"Another great eipcure is Lady Dorothy Nevill. She is always experimenting. She said to a friend, 'Guinea pig, now there's tasty dish for you. But it's always a job to make your cook do it. They want bakin' same as the gypsies serve the hedgehogs. I tried eatin' donkey too, but I had to stop that for it made me stink.' "

Mr. Booth laughed appreciatively and raised his glass. "To our good health," he said. Emily and Lord Storm dutifully drained their glasses. Emily began to wonder quite how many toasts Mr. Booth intended to go on proposing.

She was very tired, and her head was beginning to swim with all the wine she had drunk. The meal was served by Jimmy, who disappeared to the kitchens again as soon as he had set the food on the table.

And then, when Emily thought the evening would never end, Mr. Booth begged to be excused, saying he never kept late hours. They both wished him goodnight.

"I am so tired," yawned Emily when they were alone. "All I want to do is sleep and sleep and sleep."

"Then go and sleep," he said. "I shall bed down on that vastly uncomfortable-looking sofa over there, and if Mr. Booth should find me in the morning, I shall tell him I fell asleep over my cups."

Emily smiled at him gratefully. She was too tired to protest. He kissed her hand and bade her goodnight, and she was too fatigued to feel any emotion when his lips touched her hand.

Upstairs, she washed and undressed and pulled on a cambric nightgown and climbed wearily between the sheets. But she was wide awake, staring at the bed canopy, her whole body burning and aching for him. The day came back to her in restless flashes of memory. He had called her Emily. He had kissed her hand. She cradled the hand he had kissed against her cheek and longed for sleep, but it refused to come.

And then he opened the door and came in quietly, a flat candlestick in his hand. He crossed to the dressing room, the small flame of the candle casting his face into sharp relief.

"What is it, my lord?" said Emily.

He swung around and came over to the bed, his eyes in the candlestick holding a strangely brooding look as he gazed down at her flushed face and tumbled hair.

"Not asleep yet?" he said softly. "I came up to see if I had a dry cheroot in my case."

"Yes," whispered Emily, her eyes fixed on his mouth.

He gave an odd little sigh and placed the candle on the table beside the bed. He held a fold of the bed curtain back so that he could see her more clearly.

"Marry me, Emily," he said.

The strain and fatigue melted from Emily's face, to be replaced with such a glowing look of radiance that her face seemed almost luminous.

"Oh, my lord," she said, her voice catching on a sob. "Of course I will."

He sat down beside her and wrapped his arms around her, lifting her up so that she was cradled against his chest, hearing the wild beating of her heart pounding under his.

He felt as if all his senses were being assaulted, the touch of smooth satin skin, yielding, trembling lips, smells of clean hair and old linen and lavender.

And then somehow he had slung his long legs into bed beside her, lying on top of the coverlet, pressing and molding her body against the length of his own while his lips burned and moved and explored.

Suddenly, he stopped. He heaved himself up on his elbows and crouched over her, his face a blur above her own.

"I think we should wait . . . for our wedding night," he whispered.

She nodded, trying to wind her arms around his neck, but he gently freed himself and smiled down at her.

"Until we're married, my sweeting," he said softly. "Wait until then."

The morning was calm and clean and washed and fair. Mr. Booth's servants had returned late the night before, bringing with them his lordship's curricle and pair, which had been found wandering at the far end of the town. Their clothes were dried and pressed. Breakfast was eaten, and Mr. Booth soon waved them goodbye from his doorstep, reflecting sentimentally that he had never seen a married couple so much in love before.

Jimmy and Duke seemed to sense the happiness of the pair, and it was a merry party who arrived back in Somerset Square to find a much relieved Lady Bailey awaiting them in the hall.

She was delighted when Emily told her of their engagement. In Lady Bailey's mind, Lord Storm was no longer a rake, and she looked forward to bragging around Bath of Emily's conquest.

As Emily was beginning to tell her of their adventures, Lady Bailey interrupted to say that Mr. John Harris, Lord Storm's friend, was waiting in the drawing room.

"You go upstairs and change, my dear," said Lord Storm. "I'll talk to him. He has no doubt come here looking for me, since I swear he knew all along I was more interested in you than I cared to admit."

Emily and Lady Bailey went upstairs together, and Jimmy

and Duke trotted off to the kitchens to tell a fascinated audience their side of the story. Jimmy, primed by Lord Storm on the road home, altered his tale to say they had stayed the night with a Mr. and Mrs. Booth, and he made no mention of any Mr. and Mrs. Freham.

Mr. Harris rose smiling as Lord Storm entered the drawing room.

"Well, Bart, if you ain't smelling of April and May! Are congratulations in order?"

"Very," said Lord Storm, drawing off his driving gloves. "What brings you to Bath?"

"The fair Clarissa brought me to Bath, and what is more, she's going to marry me, so wish me well."

"Are you sure?" asked Lord Storm abruptly.

"Well, that's an odd thing to say. Bachelors like me don't go around popping the question every day of the week. Of course I'm sure, and I'm a very lucky man, for I thought you were quite *épris* at one time in that direction yourself."

"Not exactly." Lord Storm swung his gloves in his hand and looked anxiously at his friend. "You know, John, Mrs. Singleton was spreading some quite malicious gossip about Miss Winters around Bath."

"Oh, she told me about that," said John. "She was so open and frank about it, I tell you that's what made me fall deeper in love. She said she was jealous of Miss Winters! Fancy any woman being so noble and open as to admit a thing like that. She had tears in her eyes when she told me."

"I also believe she tried to kill Duke with poisoned chocolates," said Lord Storm, who had heard Jimmy's version on the road to Bath.

"Oh, well, actually . . . well, dash it all . . . she told me that too. I think you are being very stiff and pompous.

You can't really blame her. Fancy an ugly canine like Duke standing between you and a fortune in diamonds. Oh, do not let's quarrel. I have been waiting for you this age. Where have you been?''

So Lord Storm decided to drop the subject of Mrs. Singleton and related their adventures finding Duke and Jimmy at the fair.

Emily hesitated outside the door of the drawing room, teasing her curls in the hall looking glass. She smiled tenderly as she heard Lord Storm's voice recounting how they had stayed with Mr. Booth and had had to pretend they were man and wife because the old man was such a stickler for the conventions.

She gave a final pat to her hair and was about to open the door when she heard John Harris's mocking voice.

''So that is how you got caught, Bart! Of course, you simply *had* to propose marriage. The girl was well and truly compromised, and so were you.''

''Exactly, my cynical friend,'' replied Lord Storm.

Emily's hand dropped from the handle, and she turned and ran upstairs, and so she did not hear Lord Storm adding, ''Of course, I was delighted to be compromised, John. Somehow it was that that made me realize I was truly in love.''

Emily threw herself on the bed, her body shaking with sobs. He had proposed to her only because he had thought he must. What had been rapture for her had been simply duty to him.

Now, if Emily had thought a little more of herself, she would have been aware that Lord Storm did not have to marry her at all, since Jimmy seemed happy to keep the secret and Mr. Booth had said that he no longer went about in society. But the shame of her illegitimacy bit deep.

All at once, she knew she must return to Manley Court. For the first time she realized it belonged to her. Harriet should no longer hold sway, nor James mutter warnings of hellfire. She would take Duke and Jimmy and lock herself away behind Manley Court's tall gates until such time as she could forget that handsome, careless rake who had so casually taken her heart, and her happiness.

Chapter Seven

It was a different Emily Winters who arrived at Manley Court. In no time at all, Miss Harriet Manley found the reins of authority slowly slipping from her grasp. She should have been warned by the martial glint in young Miss Winter's eye, by the new sophistication of her dress and manner. But Harriet had been used to having her way for so long and had come to think of Manley Court as her own and Sir Peregrine's will as some kind of mad interruption to the quiet tenor of her days.

Emily was too fatigued from her journey and all the emotional upheaval to move into action the first day of her return. She took a dinner tray in her room and then spent a sleepless night, tossing and turning. Her mind cried over and over again, I am no better than my poor mother! How could I let this go so far?

Emily thought back to her hasty flight from Bath. After storming into her chamber, she had sent a bewildered maid off to the drawing room to deliver her excuse of a headache to Lord Storm.

It had been cruel to leave Lady Bailey bewildered and worried. Lady Bailey had entered her bedroom a half hour later to find Emily feverishly packing. To Lady Bailey's agitated questions, Emily had turned a deaf ear, simply saying she must return to Manley Court and she never wanted to see Lord Storm again.

Quickly, she had piled into the traveling coach with Jimmy and Duke beside her and handed a note addressed to Lord Storm to a maid. The brief, chilly note informed him that their engagement was at an end.

Hurt as she was, despairing as she felt, Emily could not help hoping to hear a thunder of hooves behind the coach heralding Lord Storm riding to demand an explanation. For a little while, she actually managed to persuade herself that he would come. Jimmy and Duke were both excited at the novelty of the journey, and the dog seemed to sense he was going home.

But as the miles passed and there was no halloa, no thudding hooves, and no Lord Storm, Emily became pale and silent, all hope gone. And by the time the tall gates of Manley Court hove into view, all she could remember was that he had said he had been compromised.

Now as she lay in her own bed, her hurt mind shrank from remembering him clearly. Had she done so, she might have realized that her beloved's besetting fault was his immense pride and that, furious and hurt as he might be over her finishing the engagement, he would no more dream of trying to see her again than he would dream of eating peas with his knife.

Harriet Manley's empire began to crumble on the following morning.

Emily entered the drawing room to find Miss Manley busy going over the day's menus with Mrs. Otley.

She stood very still and then walked forward and took

the sheets of paper with the lists of dishes from Mrs. Otley's hand.

"In future, Mrs. Otley," said Emily, "You will discuss the menus with me."

"Very good, ma'am," said Mrs. Otley, dropping a curtsy.

"Nonsense!" said Harriet. "Pay no attention, Mrs. Otley. Miss Winters has not the experience to deal with such matters."

Mrs. Otley ignored Harriet. "If you would mark the items you desire, ma'am, I will see cook carries out your orders," she said to Emily.

"This is ridiculous," sneered Harriet, quite beside herself with rage.

"Rowing in front of the servants is indeed ridiculous," said Emily coldly. "Leave us, Mrs. Otley."

The housekeeper bobbed another curtsy and then fled to the kitchens to tell the fascinated staff that miss had come into her own, and wasn't it marvelous to see that cheese-faced Harriet Manley get her comeuppance?

"Now Miss Manley," said Emily, rounding on the fuming woman, "it is quite obvious to me that this house cannot work with two mistresses. I am sure you can find other accommodations, since I am told you are not lacking in funds."

"I—I *refuse* to go!" screamed Harriet. "I shall contest the will!"

"Do that," said Emily sweetly. "But from your own address, not mine."

She then rang the bell, and when Rogers the butler appeared, which was instantly, since he had been out in the hall with his ear to the other side of the door, Emily said, "Miss Manley is leaving us today, Rogers. Tell the servants that all her bags and chattels must be out of Manley Court today. That is an order."

Harriet screamed and fumed and threatened, searching in Emily's stony eyes for some sign of weakness. But Emily remained adamant.

It was only when Harriet had stormed out that Emily began to soften a little. It must be terrible to be as old and bitter and unwanted as Harriet. Perhaps it would be more charitable to allow her a few weeks to find another home. Provided Harriet promised not to try to contest her place, Emily felt she could bear it.

She rang for Rogers again and told him she would be taking over Sir Peregrine's apartments and to tell Mr. Hardy, the steward, that she wished to see him at three o'clock in the afternoon.

Mounting the stairs, Emily reflected bitterly that her disastrous experience with Lord Storm had its advantages. It had put enough iron in her soul to deal with Harriet.

At least Duke was blissfully happy. Emily had become very fond of the dog but had to admit to herself that she was glad Jimmy had relieved her of the responsibility of looking after him. She paused at the window on the first landing and looked out over the park to where Jimmy and Duke romped in the sunlight. She took a deep breath and headed for Harriet's rooms.

Harriet was standing in the middle of her boudoir, two high spots of color on her face, directing a brace of housemaids. Five large trunks lay open, and the room was a jumble of personal possessions.

Emily opened her mouth to make her offer, but before she could begin to frame the words, Harriet began to scream and rant and rave about upstarts from the gutter seizing inheritances from the rightful owners. Emily tried to shout back, but Harriet was quite mad with rage.

Emily shrugged and turned on her heel. Harriet was leaving and that was that. One ordeal was over.

The next arrived around the middle of the day in the

shape of James Manley, who had received a message from his sister about the eviction.

Emily found him harder to deal with than Harriet; she was at first intimidated by James's clericals and seemingly pious air. But when she tried to point out reasonably that Manley Court was now hers and she would run it as she saw fit, James went into a fit of passion that quite rivaled his sister's, threatening Emily with damnation and the tortures of hellfire.

At last Emily became afraid that he would do her an injury and was forced to summon the servants to evict him.

By three o'clock, Emily was closeted with the steward, Mr. Hardy, and found for the first time that there might be a purpose in her life.

Mr. Hardy was a bluff, stocky individual, at first inclined to be patronizing, for what could a young girl know of the running of an estate?

But as Emily continued to pepper him with questions, it began to dawn on Mr. Hardy that he had a willing pupil on his hands, and he settled down to his task, explaining, showing maps, discussing what was to be done. For although Sir Peregrine had not been a very humane man, he had been conscientious when it came to the upkeep of his estates, whereas neither Harriet nor James had given a thought to it, refusing to sanction necessary repairs and failing to inform Mr. Hardy that Emily was the new owner.

Rogers interrupted them at one point to say that Miss Manley was leaving and to hint delicately that Miss Winters might find that Miss Manley was taking away a great deal from the house which should rightly stay put.

But Emily did not care what Harriet had stolen. She only wanted to be shot of her. And so she told Rogers to make sure Miss Manley was clear of the estate and then to inform the lodgekeeper that neither Mr. nor Miss Manley were to be allowed past the gates again.

She turned back to Mr. Hardy and found him watching her with admiration lurking at the back of his eyes.

Both returned to their discussion of estate business. At one point Mr. Hardy essayed a jocular remark to the effect that Miss Winters was sure to be married soon so she would not have to worry her pretty little head much longer over business matters, and he received such a bitter, quelling look that he quickly turned the subject onto the safe ground of crop rotation.

The following weeks passed busily for Emily, absorbed in getting to know her farmers and tenants. The weather was fine, and there were hopes of a good harvest.

She rode over one afternoon to visit the orphanage. But her old friends had gone, most of them to relatives who had grudgingly agreed to provide them with a home. Some of the young ones remembered Emily as their former teacher. But the orphanage only brought back sad and bitter memories to Emily, and she was glad to leave.

She reined in her horse on a little hill that afforded a view of Manley Court, circled by its gardens and parkland.

"Is that a carriage at the door?" she asked her groom.

"Yes'm," he said, touching his cap. "Spanking turnout, by the look of it."

Emily's heart began to beat hard. Could it be? She was torn between a longing to let Lord Storm—for she was all at once sure it was he—see her in her new role as mistress of Manley Court, and to spur her horse and ride as fast as she could in the opposite direction.

"Reckon we'd better be moving, seeing as you've got visitors, ma'am," said the groom. Emily weakly considered that that had settled the matter for her, and began to ride toward Manley Court.

By the time she arrived, she was so sure Lord Storm had

come calling that she brushed past Rogers in the hall without waiting to listen to him and walked straight into the drawing room.

Clarissa Singleton and John Harris rose to meet her.

Emily was flooded by such a feeling of disappointment that for one awful moment she thought she was going to break down and cry.

She welcomed her guests as best she could and rang the bell for refreshments.

"To what do I owe the honor of this visit?" she asked, eyeing Clarissa warily.

"Oh, we came for your blessing," said Clarissa lightly. "You ran away from Bath before I could see you. Mr. Harris and I are engaged to be married."

"I wish you every happiness," said Emily politely.

"We were visiting Storm, but I fear we have outstayed our welcome," said Mr. Harris with an awkward laugh.

Emily's heart beat faster. "I did not know he was in residence," she said, marveling at the calmness of her own voice.

"Oh, yes, he left Bath a few days after you. I was amazed to find that you had terminated the engagement, Miss Winters. I—"

"That is over," said Emily firmly. "It is a matter that rests between myself and Lord Storm and is no one else's concern."

"Snubbed! You have become quite *grande dame*, my dear Miss Winters," said Clarissa, laughing. "I am glad you wish us both well, for your ex-fiancé most certainly does not."

Emily gave a chilly nod, and there was an awkward silence.

John Harris was wondering rather miserably why no one seemed to adore his fiancée as much as he. He found Clarissa absolutely enchanting, but somehow his engagement had spoiled his friendship with Storm, who had retreated behind a mask of hauteur. The couple had decided to leave Lord Storm's home, where they were obviously not wanted, and journey to London so that Mr. Harris could introduce his future bride to his parents. Clarissa had insisted on calling first at Manley Court to see "her dear Emily." This had quite surprised John, because he was sure his beloved held Emily in dislike. For himself, he found Miss Winters a very cold, withdrawn sort of creature, though attractive, and he considered Storm was well out of it.

"And where is the dear doggie?" asked Clarissa brightly. "Gone to his maker at last?"

"Duke is very well. I am glad you are being honest about the purpose of your visit, Mrs. Singleton. Well, for your information, Duke is very much alive and likely to remain so for a considerable amount of time."

Clarissa arose and made a little *moue*. "Ah me," she said infuriatingly, "what it is to be disappointed in love! All thorns and prickles."

Emily touched the bell, and when Rogers entered, she said, "Mrs. Singleton and Mr. Harris are just leaving, Rogers."

" 'Fore George!" said Mr. Harris wrathfully. "You are extremely high in the instep for a . . . for a . . ."

"Don't say it," said Emily quietly. "Just leave."

Clarissa swept out, making loud and insulting comments over her shoulder to Mr. Harris, who followed. "Well, John, you said *she* broke off the engagement, but mark my words I think Storm came to his senses and is simply playing the gentleman by letting everyone think it was t'other way round. And fancy that story about Emily's having royal blood being all a hum!"

After they had left, Emily dully gave instructions that

Mrs. Singleton and Mr. Harris were not to be allowed beyond the gates again.

Then she sat for a very long time, wondering for the first time what her mother had really been like.

She walked over to the looking glass and studied her own face. It was not a peasant face, she decided. It was not low or brutish. In fact, thought Emily fiercely, I *do* look like a lady!

Emily began to pace restlessly up and down the room. An idea was beginning to form in her head. Sir Peregrine had been a malicious old man, of that there was no doubt. Only look at the cruelty of his idea of having the secret of her birth exposed before all his relatives!

Now, suppose . . . just suppose . . . he had lied about her birth. Just suppose she was not a serving maid's daughter at all! The thought was balm to her soul, which was still smarting under the humiliation of her treatment at the hands of Lord Storm.

She had a mad longing to prove that she, Emily, was born in wedlock and of noble birth. Emily was not used to indulging in fantasies, but she had been so disappointed to find that Storm had not called—so furious with herself to find that she still longed for him with every fiber of her being—that she seized on the daydream of her birth and held it close.

She would go to Dover, she would go to the Pelican, and there she was sure she would find the secret of her birth. There she was sure she would find that her mother had not been some low serving wench but a lady who had been visiting the inn.

Suddenly wild with excitement, she set in motion the arrangements for her journey to Dover. It was only when she set out some three days later with only her maid and groom in attendance that she realized she had not warned Jimmy to guard Duke with extra care until her return.

But surely with the Manleys held beyond the gates there could be no danger.

Dover lay spread out under the calm heat haze of a perfect summer's day. Gulls swooped and screamed over the sparkling sea. The town was pretty and picturesque, the Old Castle with all its fortifications on one side and on the other a chalk hill, well-nigh perpendicular, rising from sixty to a hundred feet higher than the tops of the houses.

On the south side of the town, the lofty cliff mentioned by Shakespeare in King Lear was hollowed out like a honeycomb with trench upon trench and bombproof cavern upon bombproof cavern. It had been worked a few years ago when Napoleon's invasion of England had seemed imminent, although why anyone would think he would choose that particular cliff to land on instead of, say, Romney Marsh or Pevensy Level was difficult to understand.

Anyway it had been an expensive brainchild of the ministers, who thought a brilliant idea would be to hide the English troops in these catacombs until the French had landed and then attack them from behind. It was estimated to have cost millions of pounds; there was more brick and stone buried in this hill than would go to build a new cottage for every laboring man in the counties of Kent and Sussex. It was nonetheless an endless source of conversation, and the people of Dover were quite proud to have this shining example of the stupidity of the British government to show visitors.

Emily's spirits rose even more when the Pelican came into view. It was a handsome posting inn on the outskirts of the town with an air of quiet prosperity. She arranged rooms and a private parlor for herself and her maid, noting with delight the furnishings and the quiet, well-trained servants. It seemed as if nothing—at least nothing sordid—could have taken place here.

After she had dined, Emily sent for the landlord and said she would like to ask him a few questions about the inn. She wanted to find out about someone who had been resident in the inn about eighteen years ago.

The landlord, Mr. Barret, scratched his wig and looked perplexed.

"I don't know as I can help you there, miss," he said. "I took over this here inn about ten years ago, and I don't be from Dover myself. But I believe the old owner, Jem Currie, is still living somewheres in the town."

"Could you find out his directions?" asked Emily, swallowing her disappointment.

Mr. Barret bowed and said he would do his best. It was nearly an hour before he returned. Mr. Currie, it transpired, lived in Salt Alley down by the harbor. Mr. Barrett would like to warn miss that it was not a very salubrious neighborhood, and he advised her to take her groom with her.

Emily did not want witnesses to any revelations about her past, but she compromised by taking her traveling coach and telling both coachman and groom to leave her a little way from Salt Alley and to come looking for her if she did not return in half an hour.

Salt Alley was a small, dirty, narrow, odoriferous street with a jumble of tall buildings on either side, blocking out the evening light. Emily nervously asked a slatternly woman where Jem Currie lived, and the woman took her pipe from her mouth and jerked her head to where an old man sat on a bench outside one of the dark doorways.

Heart thumping hard, Emily went forward and sat down on the bench beside him.

"Mr. Currie?" she asked shyly.

He was large and dropsical, and his clothes were a mass of stains. His dirty neckcloth was untied and hung almost to his knees, and his swollen legs were encased in dirty

bandages. He wore a dirty old Cadogan wig, stiff with
pomatum and flour and generous host to a small army of
livestock.

"Heh!" he said, turning a swollen red face on her.
"What d'ye want, missie?"

To her relief, his red-veined eyes were quite bright and
kind, and he was fairly sober.

"I believe you once owned the Pelican," said Emily.

"That I did, missie."

"I wonder if you can remember a . . . a . . . person
called Jessie Winters?"

"Jessie! 'Course I remember Jessie. Now I come to
look at you, miss, you've a look of old Jessie. A right one
she was."

Emily took her courage in both hands. "You see, I have
reason to believe Jessie was my mother. Was she, perhaps,
a lady resident at the inn?"

"Naow! Not our Jessie. Jessie was serving wench. Country girl she was. Just walks in one day and asks for a job.
No one knew where she come from. She was like you,
miss, but not like you, if you take my meanin'. Black hair,
she had, like a raven's wing, and them bold blue eyes. All
the lads were mad for her. This be awkward, miss, but is
you that there Sir Peregrine Manley's girl?"

"I don't know," said Emily miserably. "He said I was
Jessie's daughter, fathered by him."

He took her hand in his swollen red one and gave it a
clumsy pat. "Well, I'd best give you the whole story.

"This Sir Peregrine, he took a real fancy to Jessie.
Well, we all warned her it didn't mean no marriage, but
she just laughed and told us to mind our own business.
Well, he stayed a whole month and then one day he was
gone and good riddance. Arter that, Jessie began to in-
crease, if you take my meaning. I was for riding to where

Sir Peregrine lived with a shotgun, but Jessie, she shrugs and says it was as much her fault as his.

"So without telling her, I writes to Sir Peregrine and tells him that our Jessie is in the family way and what's he going to do about it?

"I thought he'd swear it was someone else's, the way most of 'em do, but he arrived one day and he just takes Jessie off, saying to me she'll be back after the child is born.

"And that's what happens. Our Jessie's dropped off at the inn some months later and she looks a bit pale and tired, like, but she says to me, she says, 'I come back to work, Jem.' And that's all. Never mentioned the babe from one day's end to the other."

"Poor mother," said Emily softly. "How she must have hated and distrusted men after an experience like that."

"What, Jessie? Naow, Jessie couldn't leave the lads alone. Three months later, she married Aaron Cobbett, plowman up at Five Elms, but he beat her something awful and she died giving birth to his child. Poor Jessie. I still mind her, laughing and joking with the fellows in the tap. There was a lot of the gypsy in Jessie. . . ."

"Everything all right, miss?"

Emily looked up and found her coachman, standing a little away, looking at her anxiously.

"Yes," said Emily numbly. "I shall leave now, Mr. Currie. Thank you for your information. Good day to you."

"And a good day to you," said the old man cheerfully. He opened his mouth to say more, but for the first time his shrewd eyes took in the richness of Emily's gown and the splendor of the waiting coachman in pink plush and glass wig. "I'm sure our Jessie would have been a great lady, given the chance," he whispered. "But you can't be a lady an' you ain't brought up to it."

Emily thanked him again. On stiff legs, she walked out of Salt Alley and climbed into the coach.

She wished she had never come to Dover. Now she would carry a picture of her mother in her head that she did not want. A mother who was a slut.

Like me, thought Emily, the hot tears streaming down her face. No wonder he did not want to marry me.

And such was her shame and misery that she quite forgot it was she who had broken off the engagement.

As her coach drove through the village of Baxtead on the last lap of the weary journey home, she saw Lord Storm.

He was seated on horseback, talking to two other horsemen. One of the men said something, and Lord Storm threw back his head and laughed. He looked elegant and carefree and heartbreakingly handsome.

Emily crouched back in the shadow of the carriage so that he would not see her, so that his eyes would not rake indifferently over her, so that he would not read in her eyes the story of Jessie Winters, the mother who had given her body away and then her baby with the self-centered lack of conscience of a common slattern.

Chapter Eight

All Emily wanted to do on reaching Manley Court was to have a hearty cry, a hot bath, and twelve hours' sleep.

But Rogers was waiting for her with the information that Jimmy had serious news and that as soon as he had heard Miss Winters's carriage he had had the boy put in the library to await her.

Jimmy was standing to attention on the hearth when she entered, with Duke lying at his feet. Duke came padding up as soon as he saw Emily, rose up on his hind legs, and planted a wet kiss on her face.

These are the only two I have anything in common with, thought Emily, fighting back the tears.

Aloud she asked, "What's the matter, Jimmy? What has been happening?"

Jimmy proceeded to unfold a shocking tale of several attempts on the dog's life. On the day after Emily had left, he had been running through the grounds with Duke, heading for one of their favorite spots, when his eye had caught the gleam of metal in the long grass just in time, and he had called Duke to heel. When he parted the grass, he had found a wicked steel mantrap carefully concealed. He had reported the matter to the head gamekeeper, who had had a squad of men search the ground and had found six more traps concealed at the spots where Jimmy usually played with Duke.

Two days later, Jimmy had been playing with Duke on the lawn at the front of the house, being too scared now to venture farther afield, when a bullet had ripped through Duke's fur but had missed the skin.

Again a search had been made of the grounds, but no one had been found; however, there had been reports in the village that the rector, Mr. James Manley, had been seen near the estate with a gun.

"Fetch Mr. Hardy, the steward," said Emily urgently. "Something must be done about this immediately."

Mr. Hardy, on being appealed to, stroked his chin and looked worried. "I don't think it's just Mr. Manley that's to blame," he said. "That Mr. Harris and Mrs. Singleton were putting up at the local inn, and Mr. Harris was laughing and joking pretty freely in his cups about how Mrs. Singleton would be wearing the Manley diamonds at her wedding.

"Now, we could hail the lot of 'em before the magistrate, but think what a scandal it would cause! And then public opinion being what it is, the lot of 'em would get a great deal of sympathy. It goes against the grain, but I think the best idea would be to *give* them the diamonds. Look at it this way," he went on as Emily and Jimmy started to protest. "The dog can't live forever and they're going to get the jewels anyway. I would suggest that Lord Storm, being executor, should be allowed to handle the matter. He can tell them as well that they're never to set foot on the grounds again, and that way Duke will be safe and we can all be comfortable."

"Can't this be done without Lord Storm?" said Emily.

"I don't really think so, Miss Winters. Mr. Summers needs to give his permission as well. It's going against the will, you know, but as long as all parties are agreed, I think we could all agree to it and all keep quiet about it."

"Please say yes, miss," said Jimmy suddenly. "That way Duke will be safe."

Emily sat down and folded her hands in her lap and thought hard. Her intellect was telling her firmly and clearly that it would be much the best thing if she never saw Lord Storm again. Her emotions, on the other hand, were weeping and crying and shrieking for just one more meeting. And then it did seem silly to live in a state of siege because Duke owned the diamonds.

"Very well," she said in a low voice. "I do not wish to see Lord Storm, but perhaps you could handle the matter for me . . .?"

"Certainly, Miss Winters. But just a point of etiquette. I think you should write to his lordship saying you are indisposed and have authorized me to handle the matter. He might not appreciate your leaving such a business to your steward without having any excuse."

"Very well," said Emily again. Would this business never end?

But there was a further irritation. A letter arrived from the Misses Kiplings, inviting themselves on a visit. Emily sent a chilly note in reply, telling them that Lord Storm would be informing them of what Mr. Summers wanted to do about the diamonds and that they would be invited then, but apart from that they were not welcome at Manley Court.

Emily was amazed at the insolence of Fanny and Betty. She wondered if they still believed her to be of royal birth

after the first shock of the news, but doubted it. Lady
Bailey had not believed the story for one minute, after
having sorted through all the possible royal personages in
her mind, and so no doubt everyone else of slower wit
would have done exactly the same thing by now.

Mr. Summers had to be written to, asking him if he
would go along with the plan and, if so, if he would fix a
date so that the Manleys could be summoned.

Finally there was a testy letter waiting from Lady Bailey
in which she wondered whether Emily had come to her
senses and realized the folly of turning down a man like
Lord Storm. There was no mention of Lady Bailey's pre-
vious opinion that the man was a rake. Then she had gone
on to complain of the morals of Duke, who, it appeared,
had seduced Lord Bellamy's pet poodle, who had given
birth to a litter of shaggy black-and-gold pups.

At last, Emily was finally able to escape to her rooms
and try to bury her hurt and worry and loneliness in sleep.

The autumn winds were whipping across the stubble
before the final arrangements were made for the delivery
of the diamonds. Emily had traveled to London to autho-
rize their removal from the bank. She stayed at her town
house for several days, venturing out only a little with her
maid to see the sights. London alarmed and bewildered her
and she knew no one in society, and so she was heartily
glad to escape back to the country.

And then the morning of the day on which Duke was to
lose his diamonds finally dawned. The Manleys, Clarissa,
and Fanny and Betty were expected at eleven o'clock. It
had been made clear to them that they were to leave
immediately after they had received their share of the
diamonds.

Lord Storm was the first to arrive. Rogers informed Miss
Winters of that interesting fact, but Emily was frightened

to see him alone and said she would keep to her rooms until everyone was assembled in the library.

At last, at exactly eleven o'clock, Rogers informed her they were all there, even Duke. Emily took a last look at herself in the glass. She was wearing a ruby-colored morning gown with an apron front and jaunty little peasant bodice laced with silk ribbons. In order to give herself an air of maturity, she put on one of the new lace caps she had ordered from London. It was made of India muslin and lace and looked very frivolous, but Emily thought it gave her the air of a dowager and was pleased with the effect. And for a single woman to take to caps was tantamount to an advertisement that she was not looking for a husband.

Emily experienced a feeling of *déjà vu* when she walked into the library. There was Mr. Summers behind the table in exactly the same clothes and wig as he had worn for the reading of the will. Harriet was sitting beside James. Neither of them looked around when Emily came into the library. Clarissa was there as before, but this time John Harris stood beside her chair. Fanny and Betty were giggling excitedly on a sofa near the fire. And Lord Storm stood over in a shadowy corner of the room.

He obviously meant to join the hunt as soon as the business was over, for he was wearing a scarlet jacket, leather breeches, and thigh-length riding boots and spurs. He gave a brief bow in Emily's direction. His eyes were blank and withdrawn.

Emily found her hands beginning to shake and quickly sat down as far away from the company as possible. Mr. Summers raised his eyebrows as he looked at her, framing an unspoken question.

"You may begin, Mr. Summers," said Emily.

"This is not of my doing," began Mr. Summers severely. "Were it not that I have a great deal of sympathy for

Miss Winters, surrounded as she is by avaricious people, I would make sure that the will stood and that not one diamond would leave the bank until the dog died.''

''Get on with it and stop moralizing,'' said Harriet, speaking for the first time.

Fanny giggled and put her hand over her mouth.

Emily decided to steal a look at Lord Storm's face and raised her eyes only to find that his were fixed on her, and so she bent down and patted Duke's narrow head.

''First, I want you all to sign this document, which says we are all agreed over the breaking of the will. If you will sign first, my lord.''

''Are you sure you agree to this, Miss Winters?'' demanded Lord Storm harshly.

''Yes,'' said Emily quietly.

He shrugged and scrawled his name. Harriet and James nearly collided in their rush to affix theirs, then Clarissa, and then Fanny and Betty Kipling.

''Sir Peregrine Manley left a letter to be read before the division of the jewels,'' said Mr. Summers. ''Dear me— the late Sir Peregrine's letters are making me quite nervous. But his instructions were very clear. I have not perused the document myself, so I cannot warn you of its contents.''

''He'll have tricked us, the old miser,'' said Harriet and received a shocked look from the lawyer.

He crackled open the parchment. ''This is addressed to Harriet and James and Mrs. Clarissa Singleton and to Fanny and Betty Kipling,'' he said, and then began to read. '' 'I'm sorry I wasn't around to see the antics of all of you trying to kill my Duke. But I assume he's dead now, and probably by your hand.' ''

''Monstrous!'' said Clarissa languidly.

'' 'So you'll have what's locked in the bank, and I hope you all enjoy them. Before my death I hope to have done something to benefit somebody other than myself. And so I spent quite a deal of money setting up a home in Kent for fallen women. You never know, Harriet, when you might need their charity.' ''

A stunned silence met this last disclosure.

Clarissa was the first to speak. ''Well, at least we have the diamonds and that interesting little piece of information that showed Sir Peregrine at least tried to atone in some way for the shame of Emily's birth.''

''Shut up!'' said Lord Storm, suddenly and savagely.

''Yes, do be quiet,'' hissed John Harris, much mortified.

Emily sat very still. So Clarissa had finally realized that the tale Lord Storm had told about her birth was all a hum.

Well, only a short time now and she would be shot of the lot of them.

As if echoing her thoughts, Lord Storm said brutally, ''For God's sake, let us get this distasteful business over. They are single jewels I believe. Open the box, man, and divide them in five and let us rid Miss Winters of our unwelcome presence.''

The lawyer opened a huge lead box. All rose to their feet as if drawn by a magnet. The box was full of cut and polished diamonds, blazing and winking in a shaft of pale sunlight.

''Make no mistakes, lawyer,'' said James, rubbing his hands in glee. ''Equal shares! Equal shares!''

Lord Storm walked across the room and came to stand over Emily. ''Why don't you leave, Miss Winters?'' he said gently. ''I shall send word when they are all gone.''

Emily's eyes flew to meet his. There had been kindness in his voice, and a sudden fluttering hope set her heart beating. But his mouth was firm and his eyes unreadable.

''Very good, my lord,'' said Emily, rising to her feet. ''Come alone, Duke.''

She turned toward the door of the library, her shoulders

slumped, Duke padding along at her skirts, peering up anxiously into her face.

A sudden scream from Clarissa stopped Emily in her tracks.

The library door flew open and Jimmy hurtled in and threw himself on Duke. He had been waiting in the hall in a fever of anxiety, fearing the terrible Manley relatives might murder Duke right under Miss Winters's nose.

"Paste!" screamed Clarissa, a stream of gems dropping from her fingers to rattle on the table. "Paste!" She swung around on Emily, her eyes blazing. "You did this. You have cheated us."

"Are you sure?" demanded Harriet, her busy hands scrabbling in the lead box.

"Of course," wailed Clarissa. "I know paste when I see it."

"There's something else here," cried Harriet. "At the bottom of the box. A piece of paper."

"Allow me, madam," said Mr. Summers, edging her aside. "It may well be another document."

Out through the glittering pile of paste jewels he drew a single sheet of paper. There was a message on it, short and to the point. He read it out.

" 'Well, you greedy lot, it's a pity I'm not there to see your faces. Yes, I sold the lot and had paste ones made instead. But you will all be glad, James in particular, to know that your loss is the home for fallen women's gain.' "

There was a stunned silence. Then the air was filled with a terrible gurgling choking sound as James Manley scrabbled at his collar.

Lord Storm bent over James and loosened his clothing, then called for brandy. Jimmy and Duke sat together in the corner, their small eyes darting this way and that.

Miss Emily Winters began to laugh and laugh.

The Misses Kipling burst into tears. Clarissa sailed

from the room without a backward glance. John Harris slumped down miserably in a chair. Harriet waited in a rigid silence until her brother was recovered and then harshly ordered him to escort her to her carriage.

Still crying, the Misses Kipling arose and followed the Manleys out. Mr. Summers sat at the table, staring at the glittering pile of fake diamonds.

Jimmy slipped from the room with Duke at his heels.

"Terrible," muttered Mr. Summers. "Your father, Miss Winters, was a wicked, malicious old man."

"But he left Miss Winters the estate and the fortune," said Lord Storm calmly, "so there must have been some good in him."

Mr. Summers waved his hands helplessly. "I fear I am quite overset, Miss Winters. Pray may I be allowed to retire?"

Emily nodded and rang the bell for a footman to show the lawyer to his room.

"I say, Bart," said John Harris miserably. "I say, old man. I don't know how to put this, but . . ."

"I think you will find Mrs. Singleton is waiting for you," said Lord Storm quietly. "I think you should leave."

Mr. Harris got wearily to his feet. "I didn't mean any harm," he said, looking from Emily to Lord Storm. "Really I didn't. Clarissa said there was no harm in trying to put a ball in the dog, and she made it seem like a game. You must understand, Bart . . ."

"Please go," said Lord Storm quietly. "I think Miss Winters has endured enough."

John Harris walked to the door of the library and then hesitated with his hand on the handle. "I say, Bart," he said over his shoulder. "I mean, can I come and see you one of these days, without Clarissa, I mean?"

"I do not think that would be in order for a while," said Lord Storm in a kinder voice. "You are to be married quite soon, and it would not be at all the thing to leave your bride.''

"Who says I'm going to be married?'' shouted John, and then, as if appalled at the loudness of his voice, he fled from the room.

Lord Storm and Emily were left alone.

"Women!'' said Lord Storm in accents of loathing. "Only see how my friend John has changed to a weakling almost overnight.''

"Do not blame women,'' said Emily. "Mr. Harris was probably always so. Circumstances highlighted his bad side, not Mrs. Singleton.''

He walked over and stood looking down at her. "So, you do not think love can unman anyone, Miss Winters?''

"That I could not tell you, my lord,'' said Emily in a flat voice. "You see, I have never been in love.''

For one minute his eyes blazed, and then he said in an equally colorless voice, "You are like those diamonds over there, Miss Winters. Hard and glittering and cold and fake!''

And with that he turned on his heel and marched from the library, crashing the door behind him with a resounding bang.

Outside in the hall, Rogers snapped his fingers and two footmen rushed to open the main door for Lord Storm.

Rogers stood for some moments in thought. Then he went down to the kitchens. Sitting by the fire, feeding Duke a marrow bone, was Jimmy. The servants approved of Jimmy, because he was quiet and well behaved and he had trained the horrible Duke to behave himself in the house.

"Come into the pantry, Jimmy,'' said Rogers.

Jimmy followed him obediently. He was somewhat in awe of the stately Rogers, who ruled the staff very strictly indeed.

"I don't believe in gossip," said the butler, picking up a glass, holding it to the light, and beginning to polish it with unnecessary vigor.

"No, sir, an please you, sir," said Jimmy dutifully.

"But a happy mistress is a good mistress, and it is in our interest to take care of her welfare."

"Yes, sir, Mr. Rogers, sir," said Jimmy, his hand automatically stealing down to pat Duke's smooth head.

"So," said Rogers, swinging around, "I would be obliged if you would tell me what all this is about Miss Winters's being engaged to Lord Storm and then breaking off the engagement."

Jimmy screwed up his face in thought. He had promised not to mention the Mr. and Mrs. Freham business, but perhaps he could tell the rest of it, and anyway, Miss Winters's lady's maid knew of the broken engagement.

"It was in Bath, Mr. Rogers, sir," he said. "Miss Winters and his lordship seemed very happy about the engagement, like. They had come down to the country to find me when I ran away with Duke. But I told you about that. Well, when we got back to that there Lady Bailey's, miss, went upstairs to take off her bonnet and my lord went to talk to Mr. Harris, what was visiting. Miss went singing up the stairs, so to speak, and changed and was that happy and told her maid all about it and went down the stairs again. John, the footman, he was on duty in the drawing room, but he says she never came in and her maid says she was up the stairs again in a minute, her face looking that dreadful, and says for to pack."

"Hum," said Rogers consideringly. "Could it be she heard something before she came into the room? Did his lordship say anything to Mr. Harris?"

"I dunno, sir," said Jimmy. "Mr. Harris said my lord was angry at him for wanting to marry Mrs. Singleton on account of Mrs. Singleton tried to poison Duke. But nothing else.''

Mr. Rogers almost absentmindedly poured himself a glass of port. ''Ye-e-es,'' he said, holding the glass up to the light. ''We must take action, boy. I would say Miss Winters feels like a sort of guardian to you.''

''She's wunnerful,'' breathed Jimmy. ''Why, I—''

''She! She? Kindly remember when referring to your betters to refer to them by name or title. Do I make myself clear?''

''Yes, Mr. Rogers, please, Mr. Rogers.''

''Very well, don't forget it. Ah, Mrs. Otley, just the lady I want to see. Now, would you say young Jimmy here was angelic-looking enough to winkle out the secrets of our mistress's heart? You know the reason for my concern, Mrs Otley?''

''Indeed I do, Mr. Rogers. Jimmy, now, let me see . . .''

She studied Jimmy for some time and then sighed. ''He's not what you would call angelic-looking. I do believe he looks like that there dog!''

Jimmy beamed.

''But,'' she went on, ''if we curled his hair and pressed his black suit and put a bit of lace around the collar and told him what to do, why, I think he would do very well.''

And so Mrs. Otley and Rogers retired to a corner with their backs to the wondering Jimmy and began to whisper.

Emily had retired to the drawing room after dining in solitary state. She had hardly touched her food; she did not know that each returned dish she sent back to the kitchens was greeted with gleeful smiles. The servants thought the untouched food was a good sign of the turmoil of their mistress's heart.

She tried to make out why she did not feel better now that she had snubbed Lord Storm, now that she had, in effect, told him she did not love him. But it had not cut him to the heart as she had hoped it would. He had merely been angry at her rudeness, that was all.

The autumn winds howled in the chimney, a log shifted in the fireplace, and the clocks lethargically ticked away the minutes.

Emily sighed. This was to be the pattern of her evenings for a long time to come, sitting alone, listening to the wind, and watching dream castles rising and falling in the flames.

The door opened and Jimmy and Duke sidled in. Emily merely glanced at them and then went on staring at the fire. It came as something of a shock when she found, a few moments later, that Jimmy was sitting at her feet, his elbow resting on her knee, and looking up into her face.

He looked quite peculiar. His scrubby brown hair had been teased into artistic curls, he wore a huge fall of lace around his neck that looked suspiciously like the hem of a petticoat—as indeed it was, Mrs. Otley having considered no sacrifice too great—and two circles of rouge had been painted on his cheeks.

He had a piece of paper, which he drew out from behind his back and looked at and then put away. "Oh, mistress dear," said Jimmy in a terrible simpering voice. "Art thou troubled in heart?"

"He's doing very well," whispered Rogers from the other side of the drawing-room door.

"Shhhh!" admonished Mrs. Otley.

"Am I *what?*" asked Emily.

Jimmy glanced at his piece of paper again and carefully put one hand over his heart. "What troubleth my mistress, troubleth me," lisped Jimmy painfully. "I wouldst lay down mine life for thee."

"*Jimmy!*" said Emily crossly. "What is this mummery? Are you having amateur theatricals in the kitchens?"

"That's blown it," said Rogers gloomily from his position behind the door.

"I knew it wouldn't work," said the second footman, James, who was of a pessimistic nature.

And the under housemaid, who prided herself on the delicacy of her nerves, burst into tears.

"And what is going on out in the hall?" demanded Emily. "There seems to be a whole army of people rustling and shuffling. You may sit here with Duke if you like, Jimmy, but only after you have scrubbed the paint from your face."

Jimmy began to blubber, and Emily looked down at him in exasperation. "What on earth is the matter?"

"They'll all b-be so disappointed in me," sobbed Jimmy. "I was for to charm the secret of your love from you, miss. We're right sorry for his lordship, seeing how badly he's in love with you and he would make a good master."

"I'll strangle that boy," muttered Rogers.

"Jimmy, dry your eyes this minute," said Emily in a stifled voice. "You do not know what you are talking about. Lord Storm does not love me."

"But he *does*," wailed Jimmy, emotion making him bold. "I know it. Everyone knows it. How come *you* doesn't know it?"

"Leave me immediately," snapped Emily. "You go too far."

Jimmy trailed from the room, followed by Duke.

Emily sat with her bosom heaving. It could not be true. If it were true, then she, Emily, had behaved abominably. All at once, she could not bear it any longer and rang the bell.

The knowledge that Miss Winters had ordered the carriage and was going to call on Lord Storm swept through the kitchens like wildfire, and Mrs. Otley left off cuffing

Jimmy and gave him a sugar plum instead—which was just as well, since Duke was about to savage her left ankle.

Lord Storm paced up and down his library. He had been hunting most of the day and had been looking forward to an evening of pleasurable fatigue. But all he could think about was Emily Winters, sitting wearing her silly frivolous cap and telling him she had never been in love.

How could she be so cruel? How could *anyone* be so cruel?

He had made a fool of himself over her just as surely as John had made a fool of himself over Clarissa.

He looked down at the magnificence of his evening dress and thought it absurd. Why go to all this trouble to spend an evening alone? He savagely kicked at a burning log in the fireplace.

And then his butler came in, looking worried. "There is a young lady called, my lord, accompanied only by her groom. She says she is Miss Winters of Manley Court and is desirous of speaking to your lordship." The butler looked meaningfully at the clock on the mantel, which was chiming out eleven o'clock.

Lord Storm experienced a sudden spasm of pure exhilaration, which was immediately followed by dark despair. No doubt she had had trouble with the Manleys and had come to him as her nearest neighbor because she had no one else to turn to.

"Show her in," he said abruptly, "and bring wine and cakes."

He leaned his elbow on the mantel, staring down at the fire. There was a low murmur of voices in the hall and then his butler announced, "Miss Winters, my lord."

Without turning around, he said wearily, "Why have you come?"

"To see you." Her voice was only a little above a whisper.

She was standing just inside the door, her scarlet cloak falling back from her shoulders. The Manley diamond collar blazed around her neck. Her gown was of fine white muslin, embroidered with a design of green silk ferns.

"I trust those diamonds are real," Lord Storm commented.

"Yes," said Emily, looking at his hard, set face and hard eyes and feeling her courage ebb away. Never had a man looked less in love.

Cakes and wine were brought in and set on a table before the fire. He dismissed the servants and poured her a glass and wordlessly held it out to her. Emily took it from him silently. Gingerly, she sat down on the the very edge of the sofa as Storm poured himself a brimmer and drained it in one gulp.

"Now, Miss Winters," he said sternly, "why have you come?"

"I—I felt I had done you a disservice by leaving Bath without explaining why I had terminated our . . . our engagement," said Emily in a rush.

"Odso? I had thought you had performed that service very well today, madam. If you recollect, you told me you had never been in love."

"I—I lied," said Emily.

He sat down suddenly on the sofa next to her, his eyes raking hers.

"Then tell me why you broke off our engagement," he said harshly.

"I—I heard you tell Mr. Harris that you were only marrying me because you had been compromised."

A faint flush crept up his face. "And that was why you went away without giving me a chance to explain?"

"I could not believe you loved me after that!" cried Emily.

"You could not . . . ? Dammit, woman, I love you with my mind, my hands, my body, my very soul. And you put me through months of hell because you were too proud to ask for an explanation?"

Emily looked at him wonderingly. "I did not think I had it in my power to put you through any kind of misery. Oh, my love, if you only knew how ashamed I am of my birth, how you seemed too good for me. I felt you were ashamed of my birth."

The hard lines of his face softened. He drew her gently into his arms and caressed the back of her neck, feeling the long shiver that ran down her body.

"I do not care anymore about your birth. I want you, Emily."

"As your mistress?"

He gave her a little shake. "As my wife, Emily. As my wife. I will even give houseroom to that damned dog, if you will only say you love me."

She looked up at him with her heart in her eyes and then threw her arms around him and buried her head in his chest. "I love you, Bart," she said, her mouth buried against his shirt frill. "I have been so unhappy."

"You have made me very unhappy too, and you shall pay for it, my love. Kiss me!"

She raised her mouth shyly to his, and he gave a low groan and began to kiss her savagely, bruising her mouth, and holding her so close she thought her bones would break.

At last his kisses became longer and more tender, sending a dizzying sweetness coursing through both of them until they forgot where they were, only burning with an insane need to lose themselves in each other.

Some time later, she lay naked in his arms in front of the library fire and said sleepily, "Why are you laughing?"

"I am laughing, my love, because we both started the

evening so miserable and so splendidly dressed, and now look at us!''

Emily seemed to come fully to her senses at last and clutched his shoulders.

''Bart! The servants! What must they be thinking?''

With a touch of his former arrogance, he looked down at her.

''I neither know nor care,'' he said haughtily. ''The charms of your left breast are infinitely more interesting. Now perhaps if I kiss it you will cease to bother with trivialities. . . .''

The servants of Manley Court sat around the table in the servant's hall. Rogers eyed the clock. ''Still not home yet,'' he said.

''I wonder if we dare hope? You see, if Miss Winters does not become married, I am sure she will soon weary of the estate and might even sell it. Now, Lord Storm would look after us. What would happen to us? There are so many bad masters, and perhaps a new owner would not want us. He might even bring his own staff!'' A low groan greeted this comment.

And then, from out in the drive, they heard the crunch of wheels.

''That'll be the mistress back,'' said Mrs. Otley. ''If only we could ask her point-blank. Perhaps Sam, the groom, will have gleaned something.''

They listened anxiously, and then at last they heard steps on the kitchen stairs and the groom came in, pulling off his cloak.

''Well?'' said everyone.

''His Lordship sent the carriage home,'' said Sam, grinning, ''and said I was to get a good night's sleep. He gave me a yellow boy and said I was to drink the health of himself and Miss Winters and he hoped I'd wish them well on their wedding day!''

What a cheer went up! Lord Storm was known throughout the county as a good and fair landlord. Their jobs were safe.

"Champagne, I think," said the beaming Rogers. "Hey, look at Duke. I swear he's as happy as the rest of us!"

Up on his hind legs, Duke was waltzing slowly around, a grin on his narrow face, while Jimmy jumped up and down.

"He's worth more'n diamonds," said Jimmy proudly. "There never was a dog in the whole wide world like our Duke!"

ABOUT THE AUTHOR

Marion Chesney was born in Glasgow, Scotland where she began her successful writing career. She has worked as a fiction buyer, a theater critic, a newspaper journalist, a book reviewer, and a crime reporter.

She has been living in the United States since 1971. Most recently she has been writing full-time and living in New York City with her author-husband and their child.